Winterbound

Books by Margery Bianco
Available from Dover Publications

THE VELVETEEN RABBIT

POOR CECCO

WINTERBOUND

Winterbound

Margery Williams Bianco

Illustrated by
Kate Seredy

Dover Publications, Inc.
Mineola, New York

Bibliographical Note

This Dover edition, first published in 2014, is an unabridged republication
of the work originally published in 1936 by The Viking Press, New York.

Library of Congress Cataloging-in-Publication Data

Bianco, Margery Williams, 1881–1944.
    Winterbound / Margery Williams Bianco ; illustrated by Kate Seredy.
        p. cm.
    "This Dover edition...is an unabridged republication of the work originally
published in 1936 by The Viking Press, New York"—Copyright page.
    Newbery Honor, 1937.
    Summary: With their parents away, city-bred teenaged sisters Kay and
Garry take charge of their younger siblings during a severe winter in rural
1930s Connecticut.
    ISBN-13: 978-0-486-49290-2 (pbk.)
    ISBN-10: 0-486-49290-7 (pbk.)
    [1. Brothers and sisters—Fiction. 2. Country life—Fiction. 3. Self-
reliance—Fiction. 4. Winter—Fiction.] I. Seredy, Kate, illustrator. II. Title.

PZ7.B4713Wi 2014
[Fic]—dc23

                                                              2013027893

Manufactured in the United States by LSC Communications
49290702   2017
www.doverpublications.com

Contents

Winterbound

The House on the Hillside

KAY had been so long hunting out her color box, and the light had already begun to change so rapidly, that she gave up the idea of painting with a little sigh and sat, instead, looking out through the window, just noting in her mind the curve and line of the October hillside, the shape of tree and branch. Outside the house, beyond the little space of flower border with its zinnias and marigolds and the bank which Garry had terraced up, dragging big stones from the pasture through hot August days, the hillside dropped away in a slope of gray bowlders and red sumac, with the old twisted butternut tree just visible above the second stone wall, the last of its yellow leaves fluttering against the blue sky. Far below came the twist of the road again, winding downhill, and behind it rose hills and more hills, a blaze now of changing reds and purples. If only, Kay thought, one could really get those colors on paper so that they looked like something alive, as they were, not just splotches of this and that, with no shape to them!

It was hard, for Kay's eye always ran ahead of her hand. She could see just how things looked, know exactly what they meant to her, but when she tried to set them down and make other people see them, too, it was never the same. The pattern always came out different. Garry even, who had no more idea of drawing than a cat, who didn't care one bit about painting except that she loyally admired everything Kay did, could take a pencil stub in her brown fingers and set down what a tree or a cow looked like, the way it was built, and though her drawing was awkward and crude there could be no mistaking that it was a tree or a cow. That, father had explained once, was because Garry was interested not so much in what things looked like as in how they were made and the way they grew; she knew that every tree had its roots solidly in the ground, it wasn't just floating in air, and that the tree's trunk and the cow's legs were that exact shape because of the weight they had to support. Her mind took after father's, that could tell from just looking at some old dug-up bone what sort of an animal it must have belonged to.

There was so much more to being an artist than merely wanting to set down beautiful things, and Kay's one year at art school had just brought her to the stage of beginning to find this out. And it was going to seem

more difficult than ever now, working by herself this
winter. For art classes had had to stop with so many
other things, and at nineteen, more perhaps than at any
other age, life suddenly seems to be slipping by so fast
that a year, even a month or a day, is far too precious
to be spent on anything except the things one most wants
to do. It was as if life were pushing one on and on and
there wasn't a minute to waste. Martin and little Caroline were all right, and even Garry, at sixteen, didn't
seem to have reached that stage yet and perhaps never
would, for there always seemed a sense of leisure about
Garry's undertakings, even when she worked her hard-
est. But Kay was all impatience. It showed in her movements, in her slim nervous build, in many ways that she
herself recognized and in countless others that she didn't
suspect.

A straight young figure in blue denim overalls passed
the window, and a moment later Garry came in, pausing
to drop an armful of fresh logs beside the hearth.

"It's going to turn cool tonight. I wouldn't wonder
if we get a frost. Did mother say what time she'd be
back?"

"I don't suppose she'll be very late. She said she'd
get Edna to drive her back if there were a lot of parcels."

Shopping, on the rare occasions when any of the Ellis
family went into town, nine miles distant, usually did

mean a lot of parcels; more than any one person could comfortably bring home by the state-road bus.

"What's for supper?" Garry asked.

"Bread and butter and fish cakes, unless mother brings something in."

"Those won't take long. We might have a cup of tea now while we're waiting. I got my cold-frame finished. I hope she remembers the putty."

"It's time the children were back," said Kay. "The school bus must have gone by ages ago. Did you see anything of them, Garry?"

"They're over at Rowe's, looking at the new calf." Garry's voice came back from the kitchen, above the clatter of pump and kettle. "It's a cute one, all red, with a white star and one white foot." She lighted the oil stove and came back to wait until the kettle should choose to boil. "Shopping is a pest in the country," she went on, shifting the wood on the fire to make it burn more cheerfully, her mind still on the cold-frame and its unglazed sash. "It isn't just thinking of what you want; you've got to think of everything you're going to be likely to want for weeks ahead. There's one thing about it; you've no chance to spend money even if you had it. Which reminds me, I found fifty cents just now in my last year's sweater pocket. I think it should go on cabbage seed for the future sustenance of the Ellis family."

THE HOUSE

"It had better go on a patch for the knees of your overalls," said her sister, "if you're really going to wear nothing else all day long."

Garry poked a brown earth-grimed finger at the tear across her knee. "Pretty far gone. The signs of honest toil. They are the only sensible wear for me, so don't grumble. If I had your figure, Kay, I might feel like adorning it. Do you remember that one time I went haywire and spent all my money on a printed georgette, and how I looked in it!"

Kay smiled. "You certainly did. No, frilly things never did suit you, you're right. You aren't the type. But I would like to design something that you would look perfectly stunning in." Her slender dark eyebrows drew together in the line that always made the family exclaim: "There—Kay's at it again!" "Brown velveteen . . ." She studied Garry's straight nose and short rumpled hair that just missed being reddish and was more the color of a ripe chestnut. "Something quite plain but very well cut. Like a fencing suit. Even trousers, if you want them."

"They've been designed already, by Sears Roebuck, only they call them pants. So all that really stands between me and perfect elegance is about two dollars fifty. Poor Kay! I know you're dying to see your whole family clothed in purple and fine linen."

WINTERBOUND

"Well, I don't see the sense of people letting themselves go just because they live in the country," Kay retorted, glancing at her own hands, well kept in spite of housework. Nothing could ever spoil Kay's hands, long and sensitive, not like Garry's square blunt fingers that seemed made for doing things and grubbing in the earth. "If you'd spend just ten minutes a day, Garry . . ."

"You sound exactly like the radio! I comb my hair—well, sometimes—and I brush my teeth. No beautiful young man is ever going to come to *me* and say 'Dearest, what I particularly admire about you is your hands! Tell me how you manage to keep them so soft and white.' Heavens, there goes the kettle!"

She returned bearing two cups, one squat and white, the other, for Kay, belonging to the pretty flowered service of which a few pieces still survived from what Garry called "our palmy days."

"I do think, as a family," she went on, settling herself in the armchair, "we showed uncommonly good sense in deciding to stick it out here. I always wanted a winter in the country anyhow and the kids will have the time of their lives. I agree with mother that the thought of going back to town and hunting the kind of cheap apartment we'd have to put up with, this winter, would be pretty ghastly. Remember those awful places we

THE HOUSE

looked at in the spring, that Cousin Caroline thought would be so nice and suitable, now that we have to 'economize' as she likes to call it? Finding this house for the summer was a godsend just when our lease ran out, and now we've got some of our own things around it begins to look all right."

"Do you suppose our unknown landlord would pay for some paint and wallpaper, as long as we're keeping the place on?" Kay wondered. "Do you think it would be any good asking?"

"Doubt it," Garry returned. "He seems a queer bird. You know when we first came up here the agent said the owner would rent the place until he needed to use it, but only from month to month. This was always the hired man's house, Neal Rowe told me, and that's why there isn't much land with it. He said he'd rent it just as it stood and he wouldn't do any fixing up, except repairs. The agent told mother he thought they were either going to pull this little house down or model it over into a guest house, when they get through fixing the big place up the hill. There was something about it interfering with their view. But that wouldn't be till some time next year, anyhow."

"It would be a shame to pull it down. I like this little house, only it does need things done to it, inside."

Kay looked round the homely low-beamed room she

had spent so much care and thought on. The old shreds
of paper had been scraped off and a coat of pale yellow
calsomine hid the cracked plaster, but that queer drab
paint still worried her. The old wide floor boards were
pretty, though the old wide cracks between them made
sweeping a burden and promised plenty of cold draughts
when winter set in. Since their own furniture arrived
from town the various odd-come-shorts with which the
Ellises had managed during the summer had been ban-
ished to the attic, all but one old blue painted cupboard
which had moved in from the kitchen, and which now
stood, with a big Chinese bowl on it, between the two
windows. If the familiar chairs and tables and the low-
back couch weren't exactly early American, as Kay would
have liked, they were plain and simple, and the chintz
curtains went all right with the yellow walls. But Kay's
real joy was the fireplace, wide and deep with its plain
paneled mantel board and stone hearth, and the real
Dutch oven at one side. No room could help but be
lovely with a fireplace like that. Every time she came
in her eyes turned to it with pleasure and it had done
much to reconcile her to spending a winter in the house.
For Kay was not fundamentally a country person, much
as she loved the beauty of hills and sky. City life and all
the things that went with it meant much more to her
than they did to Garry or the two younger ones. Some-

times those long months ahead, with only the books one already knew by heart, no picture galleries, no parties or concerts or theaters or new films, and no friends near enough to drop in unexpectedly, seemed pretty blank and dreary. Kay believed in what she called civilization, and civilization to her meant just those things. Not that there would have been much chance of theaters this winter in any case, or any concerts except those rather dull affairs for which Cousin Carrie sometimes bought tickets in a good cause, to be passed on generously to her young nieces, just as she passed on occasional dresses that "poor Emily" and the children might be able to use. But at least they would be there if one did have a chance, and there was always the feeling of being close to things, of knowing what was going on if one couldn't share in it.

Garry, who had a queer trick sometimes of knowing just what was passing in another person's mind, said now: "You're the only one it will be tough on, Kay. You'll miss your galleries and exhibitions and all that stuff!"

"It won't be for always. Though I had wanted to keep on with the League classes this year. Probably much better for me to try what I can do by myself, instead of looking at what other people are doing and getting discouraged and muddled up in my ideas." Kay spoke rather more truly than she knew, for she never came

home from a picture show without being swept by the
desire to do something that would be like something
else that she had seen there, in method at least. "And
anyway the important thing is that daddie should for
once have this chance to do work that he really enjoys,
without having to worry about how we are getting on at
home. He's never had such an opportunity before and
I'm thankful mother persuaded him to take it, and hus-
tled him off before he could change his mind."

"Yes, poor darling. Short notice is a blessing sometimes," Garry agreed. "If that other man had fallen
sick three weeks before the expedition started instead of
five days daddie would have had all that time to think
it over in. All his life he's wanted to go on a job like
this and the only chance he did get before he had to refuse. I think people should just go ahead and do what
they want to do instead of worrying about other people
all the time; that way things would work out sensibly
all around. Parents especially. You turn some perfectly
splendid chance down just because it doesn't seem to fit
in with other things and then find out afterwards you
could just as well have taken it, like the time daddie was
asked to go to Asia Minor and Martin came down with
typhoid. Scientists shouldn't have families anyway, but
if they do they ought to forget them, once in a while,
and I hope daddie will, from now on."

THE HOUSE

"What worried him is that it means a lot of extra expense and less money coming in. But if we manage all right this time he'll feel freer in the future when the next chance turns up. I wish it would be something where they needed an artist as well, though I don't suppose there'd ever be a likelihood of that," Kay sighed.

"You'd be wanting to improve on nature, and combine everything into color harmonies!" There was a sound of cheerful hooting from lower down the hill, and exclaiming, "There's Edna's car now!" Garry ran to the door.

Edna—she had a second name, but no one ever used it—had been the stay and comfort of the Ellis family ever since that first day that she drove them up from the station. She was the only woman taxi driver in that district, but the other drivers, far from resenting her competition, always had a good word for her and a friendly greeting whenever they passed on the roads. Being a shrewd person she had managed to build up more or less her own clientele. At the lake, a few miles the other side of town, there were one or two summer hotels and also a few boarding houses of the quiet old-fashioned kind where elderly people liked to stay and would return year after year. These always engaged Edna in preference to any other driver, for she drove carefully and was never in a hurry. Through catering—particularly to her "old ladies," as she called them all collectively—Edna found enough work to keep her busy through all the summer months. "They like me," she said, "because I take them for nice poky drives and always ride 'em easy over the bumps." Edna had an elderly mother herself, so she knew. In addition to her "old ladies" she took any occasional fares that might turn up without cutting into the other taxi drivers' regular business (which was why they were always ready to recommend her, in turn); she would take you into town for shopping and bring you back again, or, if you preferred, she would do your shopping for you at the charge of ten cents a store; and she was not above calling for the "help," including the colored maids, at the lake hotels and driving them in to the movies on their nights off. "They're right nice girls," she explained. "The other taxis won't bother with them so they've no way to get in and out and can't pay much anyway, and I take the whole bunch together and bring them back again at a quarter a head. If my old ladies ever got to know it I guess they'd have fits, but they never go riding after dark, so it's all right."

In appearance Edna might have been any age; she had probably looked just the same ten years ago and would look no older in ten years' time. She was New England through and through, with a quick tongue and a good sense of humor, as well as a sharp business mind. A drive with Edna was something more than a mere drive. She knew everyone for miles about, and would always toot her horn when she passed certain houses. ("Monday morning, and her wash ain't out. I bet she's off berry picking this minute!") Gossip was her middle name, and she had a fund of funny stories, for no peculiarity or odd twist of character ever escaped her. Above all Garry and the younger Ellises loved riding with Edna, especially after dark and along the back roads; her sharp eyes kept constant watch as she drove and she would interrupt one of her long stories to say casually: "There's a fox up that bank there; just watch now till I put the lights on him." And she would twist her steering wheel quickly to one side and as quickly back again, and in the momentary flash of headlights there would be the fox standing just where she said, one paw raised, his eyes shining steadily back at you from the darkness.

The two younger ones, twelve-year-old Martin and small Caroline, had heard her coming now and ran out from the Rowes' barnyard, a little lower down the road. Many drivers would have objected to two children suddenly hurling themselves at the running board just as the car was making that last steep and narrow twist on the hill, but Edna, being Edna, only shouted: "You hang on tight now, young 'uns, and look out for my paint!"

So with Martin clinging on one side and Caroline on the other the little gray Ford mounted the crest, eased itself cleverly between the big bowlder and the fence post and drew up beside the house, discharging its burden of two women, two children, and the accumulated packages of a week's shopping.

It was lucky Mrs. Ellis was fairly small, for even in the front seat she was wedged round with parcels, and had driven the last seven miles with a large white soup tureen under one arm and a parlor lamp, chimney and all, balanced on her knees, while from the rear the leg of a small upturned table threatened at every minute to poke her in the back. She disengaged herself carefully and stretched her legs with a breath of relief.

"Well, we got everything home safe, thanks to luck and Edna's driving."

"Luck is right," said Edna, reaching behind her to help hand out the bundles. "You never know what you're liable to find in a car. It reminds me of one time years ago I was walking into town in my best clothes and someone offered me a lift. There was something covered up with newspaper took up the whole floor of the car, and a pie sitting on the back seat. I'd already got one foot in before the silly fool said, 'Look out for the ice!' and sure enough I'd stepped on the ice and I slipped and sat right smack on the pie. I was never so embarrassed in my life. It was a custard pie, too," she added in afterthought.

"Mother's been to an auction!" Caroline piped, as though the fact were not sufficiently apparent.

"Wasn't it nice, there was one just outside town, and Edna took me. I got this lamp and the tureen and a little bedside stand for Kay, and a length of rag carpet, oh, and a lot of old junk and garden tools that maybe Garry can use around. And children, I found a stove for the living room! The men are bringing that and the tools and the carpet tomorrow."

"Yes, she was all set to fetch it home in the car with us," Edna put in, "but I was sort of afraid it might slip down back of the cushions or something, and we'd lose it on the road."

There was a laugh, and Mrs. Ellis said: "Edna, you're an angel on earth to bring all this truck back. I hope we haven't scratched anything for you."

"If some of my fussy customers knew the kind of things that go riding in this car when their backs are turned they'd have a big surprise," Edna told her. "This load's nothing to it sometimes."

"Take the groceries, girls," said their mother. "That parcel is meat, Martin, and the big bag is oranges. Look out, Garry, those are eggs right on top!" For Garry had seized the biggest carton and was hoisting it to her shoulder. "Edna, you can stay and have supper with us, can't you?"

"Uh-huh." Edna had two inflections for this characteristic phrase and the present one, the Ellises knew, was negative. "I promised my sister's young ones I'd take them in to the movies tonight and they'll have the house down if I'm not back on time." She climbed in and prepared to back the car around. "When that stove does come, mind you don't set it where someone's liable to trip over it without noticing. I'd kind of hate to stub a toe on it myself!"

And she drove away, as they all trooped with their bundles into the house.

The new lamp, a real old parlor relic, with pink roses round its fat china waist, was cleaned and filled, the groceries and provisions stacked in the pantry, and while Garry got supper, it being her turn for the job, Kay bore her little table upstairs to the room they shared together, where it just fitted between her bedhead and the wall. It would have to be brought down again later and scraped, she decided, for the wood underneath was better looking than the dingy pea-green paint with which it had been coated, but meantime it was ready for use, for Kay liked to read in bed and a hand lamp on a bedroom chair had been her best contrivance up to now.

It was the largest of the upstairs rooms, with sloping

ceiling and a little alcove room off it where Caroline
slept, and which in turn communicated, through a big
closet, with her mother's bedroom. Martin had the little
room downstairs next to the pantry—very handy if he
got hungry in the night—where he could come and go
as he pleased and felt himself very much the man of
the household. Anyone looking at the sisters' bedroom
could have told a good deal about the two who shared it.
Kay's side was tidy and orderly, her toilet things set out
on the bureau top, cold cream and face powder and the
bottle of hand lotion that Garry laughed at. The bed
was made just so, a strip of old embroidery and a bowl
of autumn flowers on the shelves that held her books,
and a few pictures and prints on the whitewashed wall.

On Garry's side there was one picture, an unframed
landscape of Kay's. On her bureau were a ship's lantern
and various boxes stacked one on another, and the only
jar, a wide glass one, had wire gauze for a cover and held
not face cream but two tree toads in an improvised garden of pebbles and moss. The bed was pushed against
the wall to make room for a large flat table with two
shelves above it, and shelves and table were littered with
a collection of books, old copies of the *National Geo-
graphic Magazine,* newspaper cuttings, seed catalogues,
and various zoölogical and agricultural pamphlets, the
whole comprising what Garry called her "reference

library," with an aged typewriter taking up most of the space. Being practical, she had set the table close enough to her bed to enable her to reach any of this attractive literature without too-much effort, and a nail in a convenient beam just behind her head served to hang the ship's lantern on at night.

The whitewashed walls were clean and pleasant, but their plaster showed cracks in many places and they did, in Kay's opinion, cry aloud for a pretty, old-fashioned wallpaper to cover their bareness. She reverted to the question again that evening at the supper table.

"Do you suppose he'd let us buy some, mother, and take it off the rent?"

"No," returned Mrs. Ellis promptly. "We are getting this house very reasonably as it is, and I'm not going to ask anything more. From what Mr. Roberts told us the owner is a busy man and he made it clear that he wouldn't be bothered over trifles. We'll have to do it ourselves some day or go without."

"I bet he's got loads of money," Martin put in. "Jimmie Rowe said he drove out here last spring when he was buying the place, and he has a swell car. It was a fat gray-haired man and he had another man with him. It had been raining and their car got stuck on the hill turning around and Jimmie's father had to go and help them to get out. Jimmie said he seemed kind of snooty, but the other man was all right."

"He'll probably have the place all landscaped and lily-pooled, with evergreen plantings and a concrete swimming pool." It was evident that Kay felt resentful: "I know the kind!"

"Wish he'd let me have a hand in the landscaping, before someone else wrecks it all," Garry said. She had wandered up to the low, deep-eaved house on the hill many times, and planned just what she would do with the garden if she had a free hand in it, and without disturbing the beautiful old lilac trees and syringa, and the great clumps of lemon lilies and iris that flanked the worn stone doorstep. So much could be done with that garden if only someone didn't come along and spoil it all with the wrong ideas.

"Jimmie's father says it's about the oldest house anywhere around," Martin went on. "Jimmie and I climbed in through a window one day and it's got this paneling stuff and all sorts of queer cupboards, and three staircases in it. And the chimney was all full of chimney swallows; you could hear them fluttering around."

"It certainly is a lovely old house," said their mother, "and if anyone took a fancy to buy it, in an inconvenient place like this, miles off a good road, it's probably because they like the place for itself and wouldn't want to spoil it, though I don't suppose that simple thought ever entered your heads. To hear you girls talk, anyone might think you had the monopoly of all the good taste there is in the world."

"But we have, Penny darling, we have," Garry exclaimed, "and you know it perfectly well! It's all part of the general brilliance of the up-and-coming young generation—just in the air, you know. Nobody hides their light under a bushel these days."

"An old-fashioned pint pot would about cover your light very well, and you needn't call me darling, either," retorted her mother.

Garry was unabashed.

"Penny always feels guilty when she's been to an auction," she explained to the table generally, buttering herself a last slice of bread. "And then she takes it out on us poor innocents. It's very hard to be young *and* unappreciated."

Small Caroline had listened to all this with a grave and preoccupied air. She slid from her chair now and stood for a moment gazing into space.

"Mother, what did Edna mean when she told you to be careful not to trip over the stove?"

Coming on top of Garry's remark, this made Mrs. Ellis blush unaccountably.

[22]

THE HOUSE

"She meant that a stove is a very hard and unpleasant thing to stub your toes on, and as you are the person who does most of the toe-stubbing around here, she was probably thinking of you."

"But she said *you*," Caroline persisted.

"She meant all of us. Now if you've finished your supper you can go out and play till it's time to dry the silver."

"Can I go over and play with Shirley?"

"You can not. You can play in the yard."

"I wish I could go and play with Shirley!"

"If you spend any more time in wishing," said her mother pleasantly, "it will be too dark to play anywhere, and then you'll have to go to bed."

Caroline trailed half-heartedly towards the door, as Kay and Garry began to gather up the plates.

"There's one of you, anyway," said Mrs. Ellis, "that's going to be brought up right."

A muttered sound reached them, and she added aloud: "What was that you just said, Caroline?"

Caroline faced round, her hand on the screen door. "I only said 'shucks!'"

Kay smiled, and Garry turned to her mother.

"You see, Penny dear—you'd far better give it up! It isn't the least use in the world!"

[23]

Listeners Hear No Good

"MOTHER, Mr. Rowe's going to take apples over to the cider mill. Can we go with him?"

"I don't know if he wants you . . ." Mrs. Ellis began.

"He does," Martin insisted. "He saved it for Saturday so we could all go along."

"Is Shirley going, too?" For Caroline was hopping in the background, as impatient as her brother.

"Yes. Her mother said she could!"

"Then run along! Caroline, you'd better take a coat."

They dashed off down the road to where Neal Rowe was waiting with his dilapidated truck, already loaded with two empty barrels and the heaped apples, a mountain of them, red and yellow and speckled, that Martin and Jimmie had helped all morning to rake up under the orchard trees. Shirley and Caroline sat in front and the two boys climbed in behind, hollowing a nest for themselves among the apples and holding to the sides of the truck as it lurched and swung down the bumpy road.

It was a clear day, with a sky of that deep burning blue that only comes in fall, and a tang of brush smoke and wild grapes on the air. Virginia creeper and poison ivy were scarlet along the stone walls, and asters and golden-rod still bloomed here and there by the roadside. The mill to which Neal always took his apples was not the big affair down the state road but a smaller one some few miles away, reached by a narrow back road that wound up and down hill, now through woods, now between stony pastures thick with sumac, becoming less and less traveled as it went, till at the last dip it joined the beginning of an old corduroy road crossing a tract of swamp land.

This road had originally been built for logging. Years ago all the big timber had been cut from the swamp and now there was only a sparse second growth, with the old water-logged stumps dotting the ground and here and there a dead tree, gray and gaunt like a skeleton, and everywhere the rank emerald swamp growth thrusting up through the black spongy soil. The air was close and heavy with the smell of rotting wood and stagnant water. There was a legend that bears lived—or had lived—in this swamp, which stretched on either side for a couple of miles, and Jimmie and Martin felt an excited thrill as they peered between the trees, while the little girls pressed close together, staring down fearfully at the dark water that oozed between the logs as the truck pushed slowly forward.

"Don't know how good this road is any more," Neal said as he steered carefully, watching his front wheels. "It's all of a year since I was over it last. If the old truck gets stuck, boys, you'll have to help pull her out!"

But the old truck didn't stick, for the swamp water had preserved the logs and the corduroy road, though broken in places, was still good for a long time to come. Soon the skeleton trees and dead stumps gave way to thick undergrowth, alder and scarlet swamp maple, the corduroy to a firmer wagon road, and with the wayside bushes brushing the windshield as the truck forced its way through, they came out again into open country.

"There's the old house I was born in, and where I lived most of the time I was a boy," said Neal, pointing presently to a gray weathered frame house with a red barn near it. "There's the same old woodshed, and the same old pump where I drawed water many a time."

He slowed up to wave to a youngish man who was splitting wood outside the house.

"Hello, Neal!"

"How's the folks?"

"Fine. Takin' your apples over?"

"They ain't much good this year. I figure we might get a barrel out of the whole lot. Where's Bert?"

"Over to the mill. They been workin' there all morning. Guess they'll be able to put yours through now."

"Gid-dap!" said Neal, addressing the truck.

Two little girls who had come out from the house door stared gravely at the truck and its passengers. The four children stared back. There was a lurch and Martin clutched at the rolling mound of apples behind him. They rode on, turned at a crossroad. The roofs of buildings showed between the trees. They had reached the cider mill.

In spite of early morning frosts the weather had still held so mild that Garry found plenty to do yet in the garden. She had set the missing glass in her cold-frame, built from a few boards and some old sash found in the cellar and set in a sunny angle by the woodshed. She was sowing cabbage, cauliflower, and lettuce in one side to come up early in the spring, and in the other seeds for the flower garden she still hoped to have next summer. By a contrivance of her own involving various boxes of earth, some old matting, and a considerable portion of the floor space in that part of the shed adjoining the kitchen, she planned to keep the family supplied with salad and fresh parsley during the winter, little realizing as yet what a Connecticut winter could be like.

The famous living-room stove had arrived the day after the auction, and Edna's dark hints were explained. Requiring the efforts of two men to transport her piecemeal from the truck to the spot where she now stood finally assembled, Big Bertha, as the Ellis children had instantly christened her, belonged to the days when stoves were stoves. Towering and immense, she took up the whole hearth, all but blocking the fireplace that had been Kay's joy. No modern simplicity of design about Bertha. She was ornate and dreadful, with scrolls and curlicues everywhere about her. Her bulging cast-iron sides displayed a design in high relief, strikingly inappropriate, of storks wading on one leg amid a lake of bulrushes, while her summit, overtopping Mrs. Ellis's head, was graced by a strange ornament resembling a lopsided funeral urn. But hideous as she was she promised warmth and comfort; she had already an air of presiding over the family welfare, and Mrs. Ellis, feeling guiltily responsible for her looks, defended her warmly.

"It isn't so easy to pick up a good second-hand stove like that at the beginning of winter, and looks aren't half as important as comfort, if you can't have both. If you ask me, we're pretty lucky. . . ."

But here she was obliged to stop, for Penny's comment

in almost every situation involving minor doubts or criti-
cisms usually began, "we're pretty lucky"—and the
phrase had become a household word.

"It wouldn't be so easy to pick up that stove any time,"
Garry agreed, and Martin giggled promptly.

"Garry might bring some of her boxes of earth in
here, and we could train morning-glories up it," Kay
proposed sarcastically. "They'd go well with the storks!"

But Caroline had the most practical suggestion.

"We could fence off the fireplace in back with chicken
wire and raise baby chicks there. Shirley said they knew
a woman and she raised baby chicks in her fireplace all
winter, and they slept under the stove to keep warm."

"Heavens!" cried Garry. "Can you see Big Bertha
hatching out a family? How would you like a lot of
little chicks running about on cast-iron legs?"

"I said *back* of the stove," retorted Caroline, who was
extremely literal-minded. "And I don't see why you always make fun of me when I have an idea!"

So far the first official kindling of Big Bertha had
been put off, for it was still possible to use the fireplace,
even though obscured by her portly presence, and when
the logs were blazing and she stood silhouetted against
the glow the effect suggested a fat hippopotamus bask-
ing genially in the warmth.

On the afternoon that the children drove to the cider

mill Garry took a basket and went up the hill for frost grapes. It was a bit late to gather them, but Mrs. Rowe had said they were good for jelly, and Garry knew where there was a big vine, not too high for easy reach, for as a rule frost grapes are like squirrels and cling to the highest branches. She climbed the rise behind the house, crossed two steep pastures, and sat down on the last stone wall to rest and gaze about her. The sun lay warm on the lichen-covered rocks, a woodpecker was busy on a dead chestnut tree close by, and a chipmunk slipped out from a chink in the wall, ran a few inches in his curious jerky way, exactly as if he were being pulled on a wire, Garry thought, stared at her and slipped back again.

How could anyone want to live anywhere but in the country, she wondered, her eyes resting on the valley below her, on the long roof of the old house set among its yellowed maple trees and on the smaller gray roof below it, with smoke curling up from its chimney, a gray wisp on the clear air. Out here it was as though the city did not exist, and so far as Garry was concerned it could cease to exist forever, for she had none of Kay's hankerings for city life and comforts, and it never cost her a moment's concern whether the daily paper arrived by the noon mail or not, except for the one day in the week when it had gardening news.

If Garry had any definite ambition beyond the present it was to be a scientist like her father, to go on expeditions, to explore, Central America or anywhere else, it didn't matter, so long as it was wild. She devoured travel books whenever she could get them and liked to pore over the Atlas. But she was interested in live things, not so much in prehistoric ones or the remains of dead civilizations. She saw life, the whole world as it were, stretching out immeasurably in all directions, radiating from that one tiny unimportant focus which was herself, Margaret Ellis. It was all there, she was just at the beginning of it. There was no hurry at all. It was a play which might begin at any moment. Sooner or later things would happen. Meantime she had the happy faculty of being able to live in the moment and to become very thoroughly engrossed in present interests. Gardening was the chief one. She liked things that she could touch with her hands, plant and tend and make grow. She liked to dig in the earth, handle stones, drive nails into wood, and whatever she did she did thoroughly. It was a family joke about Garry that at nine years old, having been given a small skin horse for a birthday present she had taken her weekly dime to the secondhand bookstore she passed on the way to school where in one of the outside bargain boxes lay a pile of remaindered copies of a veterinarian handbook entitled: *The Horse: Its Care in Sickness and Health*. The old bookseller, who had noticed her poring over this work more than once, was so amazed by her choice that he gave her a copy and refused the ten cents for it, and for months after the six-inch steed was housed, fed, groomed, and tended strictly according to the advice in the paper-covered volume, enjoying more sickness than health in the process; for the book contained so many interesting accounts of disease and accident that Garry put him through all in turn, including spavin, glanders, and wrenched shoulder.

Later it was always Garry that the younger children turned to when baby sparrows were picked up in the park, when the guinea pig had colic or the kitten got a bone stuck in its throat, for she kept her head in emergencies and if she didn't always know what to do concealed it by a competent and reassuring air which, with common sense, went a long way towards saving the situation.

With a comfortable stretch she picked up her basket now and set off for the grapevine. The thick tight clusters hung in profusion, dead ripe and beginning to shrivel, sharp and rough to the tongue but filling the air with their wild heady perfume. There were plenty of briars too growing near, and Garry's bare brown arms were scratched and her shirt torn by the time she had forced her way into the tangle to reach the last dangling bunch that the basket would hold. There were still plenty left to be reached by a little climbing and yanking; she would have to come back tomorrow and bring a bigger basket, although this one was pretty heavy by the time she had packed all the grapes in and pressed them down.

The shortest way home was to follow the stone fence for a little distance till she reached the gap, and then down across the orchard behind the big house. The long grass under the apple trees was strewn still with fruit —none of it very good, Garry decided as she picked up an apple here and there, bit into it and threw it away. The trees needed pruning; they had been neglected for too long.

As she neared the house she remembered what Martin had said about the unfastened window. She set her basket down under one of the big lilac bushes by the kitchen door, deciding to investigate. All the windows on this side seemed tightly closed; she could see nails driven on the inside, just above the lower sash; the old country way of securing an empty house when there are no window locks. A lean-to woodshed barred her way at the end but the door stood ajar. She pushed it open. An old chopping block, some empty paint cans and a barrel, odds and ends of rusted iron—the sort of litter that seems to remain in the woodshed year in, year out, though families come and go. And at the farther end, another door.

Garry never expected it to give to her touch, but it did.

"That's one on Martin," she thought triumphantly. "This was probably open all the time!"

There is always a queer feeling about a house that has stood empty for long, especially an old house. The silence in it is deeper than the silence outdoors. One feels the hush not only of the room one is in but of all the other rooms as well, as though the house itself were listening. Without meaning to, Garry found herself treading on tiptoe as she moved.

This was the kitchen, with the big old pantry off it. The living room was beyond, across an entry where stairs went up. There was the paneling, just as Martin had said, and the queer cupboard high in the wall at one side of the big fireplace where a blackened crane still swung below the chimney. How Kay would love this room, and the smaller parlor off it, with its built-in painted corner cupboard! Garry knew enough to tell that the iron latches and hinges on doors and closets were as old as the house itself, and that the irregular split-looking nails which held them in place were the old "butterfly" nails, handmade like the latches themselves.

Kay must come up here sometime, but meanwhile Garry was determined to explore every corner first herself. Such a chance might not come again. She tried another door, and found a twisting staircase that led to a wide landing. More rooms up here, all opening one from another, built around the enormous chimney that took up the whole center of the house. The last one in the chain led back again to the landing, but there must be others beyond, and Garry was just wondering what door she might have overlooked when to her horror she heard footsteps downstairs, and the sound of voices.

She moved as noiselessly as she could to a front window and peered out. Yes, there was a car, and a girl of about her own age in a white sweater and beret just turning back from it, a parcel in her hand. Probably they had all been out in the garden when she entered the house, and coming from the back she had never seen the car; the house would have hidden it. Just the sort of fix I would get into, Garry thought, as she backed cautiously away and stood listening, wondering just what chance she had of slipping out again unnoticed. Mighty little; these old wide floor boards were sure to creak and it seemed to her that one could have heard a pin drop from one end of the house to the other.

The light measured footstep below sounded startlingly clear now, and a woman's voice, with an odd foreign lilt to it, exclaimed: "Yes, it is all beautiful, but my poor Charles, you were crazy! You will have to spend a fortune on this place to fix it up. Think of all there is to be done!"

"But Gina, think of the swell time we'll have doing

it!" returned a deeper voice, evidently that of poor
Charles.

"Look—I ask you just to look—at that ceiling! The
plaster is ready to drop."

"Look at those old latches!"

So someone at least appreciated the latches. Remembering her mother's remark—funny how Penny was so
invariably right— Garry felt a sudden liking for poor
Charles, invisible below her.

"Yes, all that is lovely," Gina went on. "You are
really very lucky, Charles. Not a thing here has been
spoiled. You know, sometimes you find an old house like
this and everything in it has been taken—everything.
And now that there is this rage for old things and anyone
will buy, you just cannot trust these country people.
They are all the same, everywhere you go. If it were me
I would lock this house very well when you leave."

"You would, would you!" Garry reflected. "Nice for
me! And what do you know about country people, anyway?" Poor Charles might be all right, she decided, but
this Gina, whoever she was, had altogether too much to
say.

"We'll go round all the windows, just to please you,
before we close everything up."

"Even the latches they take, and the hinges off the
closet doors. Anything that will bring a price. I am

quite serious. Amy Vankirk, who just bought a house in the Berkshires, told me."

"Yes, all one needs in the antique business these days is a light truck and a house wrecker. I've thought of going into it myself, some day."

"You laugh, but even you wanted to steal an old rusty lantern hook the time we picnicked in that barn, only it wouldn't come out."

"Set a thief to catch a thief! I shall have to search you, Gina, before you leave these premises."

"Ah, but I have no pockets—see?" Her laughter was swift and musical. Again Garry heard her pacing the floor. "Your old furniture will go nicely here, and there is good space for your pictures."

"There's space for dancing, in this room. These boards would wax all right." That must be the younger girl. "We ought to have parties here, and lots of people. The fireplace will be grand to sit around. Let's have a big Halloween party here next year!"

"If your friends ever arrive to see you, up that hill. Never will Uncle Maurice forget that time that you stuck in the ditch like two sillies, and the people had to pull you out with horses! He talks of it yet."

So the snooty man was Uncle Maurice. Well, served him right; he shouldn't try to bring expensive cars up back roads in the spring.

"Well, it wasn't so bad today. And the town should do something towards that, another year. I'll have to speak about it," Charles decided.

"I like country roads, they'll be splendid for riding. Charles, we ought to have saddle horses here! There's the barn to keep them in." It was the easy happy voice of a girl who had never had to worry or wonder where money came from, and Garry felt her first little twinge of jealousy, for riding was one thing she had always longed to do. "I wonder what sort of people live around here?"

"I don't know and I don't care. You can find that out for yourself." Charles sounded cheerfully indifferent. "I expect to be too busy to bother about them. There's a family down the road."

"You mean the small house you have rented—the *contadini* house?" This was Gina's precise voice. "That will be so close to us, here! Tell me, what sort of people are they?"

"I don't know. Roberts rented it to them. There's a bunch of kids, I believe. Some family from the city that wanted a cheap place."

Listeners hear no good of themselves, Garry reflected, edging none the less a little nearer to the landing.

"Cheap city people . . . but that sounds detestable. You should never have left it to him, Charles. I would prefer that they were really *contadini*—what you would call peasants."

Cheap city people! If anyone were detestable, Garry thought, it was this Gina woman. But Charles's voice broke in:

"I would do nothing of the sort, and if you go talking of peasants around here, my dear sister-in-law, people will probably think you mean something to shoot."

The younger girl giggled, but Gina returned calmly: "At least you can get rid of them quite easily; you have only to say that you need the house."

Garry's ears were burning but it was her own fault, she told herself grimly; if she didn't like what she heard it was just too bad. But that "cheap city people" still rankled. If only they would go outside again, and give her a chance to escape!

"Jane, where is Suzanne? She has run off again. Go and call her; we must go, Charles, it is hours to drive! But I just want to look at the upstairs once more."

"That settles it," said Garry to herself. "Might have known I wouldn't get a break. Wants to make sure where they're going to put the tiled bathrooms in, I suppose. How about just stepping out and saying I'd dropped in to look over the house? But I'd never get away with it; not with that Gina woman. Better beat it, quick!"

But where? Suddenly she remembered the woodshed

ell. There must be a room somewhere at that end. Her feet crunched loudly on some fallen plaster, but it was too late to worry about that as she sped on tiptoe, making for the far end of the house. By luck she found what she had hoped for, a small room with a window giving on the woodshed roof. The window was nailed, but insecurely; in a moment she had wrenched it loose, pushed up the sash as noiselessly as she could, and slipped through.

As she dangled for an instant, her legs over the edge of the shingles, she heard a peculiar and smothered sound below. A small snubby face, with bat ears and bulging scandalized eyes, stared up at her, undoubtedly the missing Suzanne. There was a moment of suspense; then the yelp that had been visibly gathering died in Suzanne's throat. Evidently the sight of Garry's overalled legs, hanging as it were from heaven, struck terror to her small-dog soul. She gulped and fled.

Garry let herself drop, snatched her basket, and dodged through the overgrown bushes to the orchard. A moment later, the basket on her arm, she was strolling with careful indifference down the road past the house.

Turning her head, she could see the young man standing by the car, his back turned to her. Too bad; she would have liked to see at last what poor Charles really looked like. Gina was still invisible, but Suzanne was there, still suffering under a sense of outrage and yelping hysterically at the girl in the white beret. But small dogs fortunately can tell no tales.

The children returned from their expedition at dusk, Martin carrying a gallon jar of new cider and Caroline a smaller brown demijohn to be put aside for vinegar, gifts from the Rowes. They were full of all they had seen on the drive, Martin especially. They had gone through the famous swamp, they'd stopped at a house where an old man had two tame coons in his corncrib; they had watched the apples being crushed, and the mill was worked by a gas engine like the one Neal used to saw wood, and they had drunk the fresh juice in tumblers as it ran from the press. It was good, Martin said, but not very fizzy yet. Neal Rowe had said it couldn't hurt anyone, it was just like drinking fresh apples.

Nevertheless it became evident, from Caroline's increasing air of aloofness, that all was not entirely well within; she refused supper, let Martin do most of the talking, and only roused once to say with an injured air:

"Shirley drank just as much cider as I did, and I don't see why she hasn't got just as worse a stomach ache as I've got!"

"How do you know she hasn't?" Kay asked.

"I *know* she hasn't, because I asked her coming home on the truck."

[42]

"I expect she is more used to it than you are," Mrs. Ellis suggested.

"If you ask me, you're both of you little pigs," said Garry with sisterly bluntness. "Martin hasn't got any stomach ache."

"Martin's a boy," Caroline returned, as though that settled the question. "It don't matter what boys eat an' drink!"

"If I did have I wouldn't talk about it, anyway," Martin told her, conscious of an uncomfortable tightness about his own waistband but unwilling to admit it. "If you aren't careful, Caroline, it might all turn to vinegar inside you, because that's what cider does when you leave the cork out."

"Then I should think you'd some of you might have told me about it before I went!" Caroline sniffled, and was led off to bed with a hot water bottle for comfort.

"The new people were up at the house again today," Kay announced as the two girls were washing supper dishes. "Mrs. Rowe saw them drive by."

"Yes? I thought I noticed a car there, coming home."

"What's the joke about it?"

"Oh, nothing. Sometime maybe I'll tell you."

And that was all Garry would say.

Across the Road

AFTER Thanksgiving the weather turned suddenly cold—a sharp businesslike cold, with an air of having come to stay. "Nearly an inch of ice on the rain barrel this morning," Garry would announce cheerfully, warming her chilled fingers as she watched through the window four bobbing heads in woolen caps—Shirley and Caroline, Martin and Jimmie—hurrying down the hill to catch the school bus. Big Bertha did her duty nobly, though her huge stomach seemed to consume as much wood as might run a locomotive until Mary Rowe, slipping over one morning to borrow some coffee, gave them a lesson in the proper setting of drafts.

"Wood stoves are all right," she said, "but I guess you've got to be brought up with them to know their ways. There—now your heat'll go where it belongs, not all up the stovepipe."

"Does it often get much colder than this?" asked Kay, who was the shivery one of the family.

"Colder?" Mary Rowe laughed. "It hasn't started to get cold yet! Why, I haven't even looked out the children's heavy underwear. You wait a bit!"

She looked anything but wintry herself, with slim bare ankles above her keds and only a thin windbreaker over her cotton house frock. "I guess this house ought to be pretty comfortable for you. It was when we lived in it."

"I never knew you lived here," said Garry.

"Two years, before we bought our place. Before Shirley was born; Jimmie was a baby. The hill keeps the north wind off, but you'll get it from the south, and that's a mean wind in winter. How are your windows, pretty tight?"

"They were drafty yesterday," Mrs. Ellis told her. "That wind seemed to come in everywhere!"

"It's the old sash. I'll get Neal to look at them." She went over and held her hand against the window sills, here and there. "Feel that? I tell you what you do. You get strips of newspaper and fill in all those cracks, poke it right down; that'll make a difference. There's plenty of little tricks to make a place comfortable, only you've got to know them. If you live in the country long you soon learn!"

Next to Edna, of whom they saw little these days, the Rowes were rapidly becoming the mainstay of the Ellis family. Besides fixing the windows and planning the doors—details which hadn't mattered so much in warm weather but were important now—it was Neal who helped them bank the house with leaves and earth on the north side and nail over the woodshed cracks; Neal who cut and hauled their cord wood for them and sawed it up, not with the gas engine which, like many of the Rowe possessions, had permanently broken down—"giv' up the ghost," as its owner cheerfully remarked—but by means of the faithful truck harnessed to an improvised saw table, till there rose in the side yard a mountain of stove wood which the Ellises innocently imagined would more than last them all winter. It was Mary who advised in all household emergencies and who came miraculously to the rescue—dropping everything to dash bareheaded across the road the time their stovepipe caught fire, which it inevitably did before long, they having supposed that all one needed to do with a stovepipe was to set it up and leave it there.

Martin and Caroline made no bones about preferring the Rowe household to their own. Jimmie was just a year older than Martin, while Shirley and Caroline could almost share birthdays. To see the two little girls together one might easily have taken pink-cheeked Caroline for the country child, for she was far sturdier in build, Shirley being slight and fair, with a pointed elfish face, upturned faintly freckled nose, and gray dark-lashed eyes

[47]

that looked too big for the rest of her features. While she and Caroline sewed, played dolls, and kept house, Martin and Jimmie were deep in their own plans and occupations. They spent evenings poring over the mail-order catalogues and knew by heart every item in the saddlery, gun, and hunting pages, their chief interests at this moment.

The two were well matched. Jimmie owned a .22 rifle and could be trusted with it, since he took hunting seriously and would have scorned to shoot at a small bird or a squirrel; he had a born instinct for woodcraft and knew the name, habits, and ways of every bird and beast around, while Martin, though he had never handled a gun in his life, had more than the average boy's knowledge of natural history, and moreover owned a father who knew all about prehistoric animals and dinosaurs' eggs and was at this very moment away on a scientific expedition in Central America—enough in itself to invest him with an aura of magic and importance to Jimmie, who had never seen a museum or zoo in his life, had access to few books, and had long ago exhausted all that the school library could offer on the subject nearest to his heart. When the two boys were not outdoors together or confabulating in their special corner of the Rowe kitchen they were usually shut up in Martin's room at home, deep in his model engine or his microscope, possessions which had taken on new interest since this friendship began; while all Martin's books in turn found their way across the road in exchange for copies of cowboy stories and other periodical Western literature.

The Rowe kitchen had a special attraction for the younger Ellises. There were other rooms in the house, including all upstairs and the parlor with its old furniture, braided rugs on the oak floor, and a case of stuffed humming birds on the mantelshelf, but compared with the kitchen they might as well have been non-existent. It was in the kitchen that family life centered. It was a long low room (the Rowes, being country people, had preferred to keep the largest room in the house for its original use) with the stove at one end, flanked by a piled wood-box on one side and an old comfortable sofa on the other, set back in a sort of alcove and wide enough for the little girls to play house there of an afternoon and for three-year-old Tommy to take his midday nap on in cold weather, tucked under a patchwork quilt. Behind the stove the old chimney-breast bulged out, making a wide shelf on which the boys liked to sit dangling their legs and watch whatever was cooking on the stove top. An old pine dresser and a chest stood along one side of the room; on the other, Mary's house plants occupied one sunny window and her sewing machine another. At the far end a row of outdoor coats hung from pegs, with a jumble of rubbers and boots below them, and Neal's rifle and an old shotgun leaned in the corner next to the back door. Either Sam, the old black-and-tan foxhound, or Dolly, half hound, half pointer, usually lay stretched under the table in the middle of the floor, safe there from being trodden on or stumbled over, while Jimmie's Ranger, a brown-and-white nondescript and the best woodchuck dog in the neighborhood, shared with three cats the warmer refuge under the stove.

Here, when schoolwork was finished, Martin liked to spend his evenings, discussing plans with Jimmie in the sofa corner, reading at the table under the kerosene lamp, or, if Neal was in a talkative mood, listening to the hunting tales he would tell them as he lounged in the big wooden rocker, pausing now and then to reach out to the wood-box for a fresh stick to put on the stove, while Mary Rowe, who never seemed to sit down except at meals and not always then, moved on errands of her own about the room or just stood, to join in the talk.

Garry, too, like the Rowes' kitchen, for it was a room she felt thoroughly at home in, and Mary shared her own eagerness about gardening and flowers—especially wild flowers, and would drop whatever she was doing at any moment to look something up in the botany book or to exchange descriptions of plants she had seen or knew, and whereabouts they were to be found. She and Neal between them had at their fingertips, too, the history of every old house, abandoned or occupied, for miles around, of the people who had lived in them and of certain queer things that had happened there, stories just as exciting to Garry as hunting tales were to Martin.

Martin was there one evening—Caroline too, for the next day was a Saturday—when Neal, who had been working late, came in, bringing a draft of cold air with him from the opened door.

"Going to snow before morning," he said, hanging up his leather jacket and coming over to the stove. "You can smell it coming, on the air."

"About time," said Mary. "We've had one or two flurries but no real snow yet. Generally it comes earlier than this. Want some supper, Neal? It's right in the oven here."

"I had some over to George's. They were just sitting down to it before I left. But I could do with a slice of that apple pie, if you've got any left, and a cup of coffee. And I guess the boys could, too—hey, Martin? Jimmie I don't have to ask, nor yet Caroline there; she looks like she could eat pie any hour of the day. I guess they don't feed you right, over home. Kind of wasting away, you are!"

Caroline, never quite sure whether Neal was making fun of her or not, said she guessed she wasn't hungry, thank you, and sat up a little stiffly on the sofa. But the big coffeepot on the stove was full, there was just pie enough to go round, and Caroline relented when she saw it and shared a plate with Shirley, each drinking in turn from the white cup that held more hot milk than coffee.

The last of the pie had just vanished when Neal, who was rolling a cigarette, turned suddenly, the half-filled paper between his fingers, and old Sam, who had been asleep under the table, lifted his head.

"Hear that?"

From somewhere outside the house there sounded a strangled scream, followed by a horrible blood-curdling wail that made Caroline turn white, while even Jimmie jumped in his chair and Martin's mouth hung open.

Neal looked from one to the other, smiling.

"I bet *that* scared the life out of you, huh? Just take a look at Shirley!"

If anything could have made Shirley's eyes any bigger it was the sound she had just heard as she sat there trans-fixed.

"Cheer up, Shirley, it's nothing but an ole gray fox hollerin'!"

Martin drew breath.

"It . . . didn't sound like a fox. It sounded like . . . like someone being killed! I thought foxes barked."

ACROSS THE ROAD

"They do. Red foxes bark. But the gray foxes, they just holler like that sometimes." Neal crossed the floor softly and threw open the back door. "Keep the dogs back, Jimmie, and give me the flashlight. He must have been right back of the house here somewheres."

The boys pressed close beside him in the doorway as the flashlight played here and there on the dark yard, the dim sides of barn and outhouses. The cold fresh air drove past them into the kitchen where the two little girls sat on the sofa, listening.

"Did you shut the chickens up all right, Jimmie?"

"Sure, Dad. Guess he came down nosin' around the garbage dump."

Shirley was peering anxiously under the stove, where the three cats still slept undisturbed.

"Gray foxes *get* cats," she said in a scared whisper.

"They eat them?" Caroline looked horrified, as well she might.

Shirley nodded. "If they catch 'em outside they do, sometimes. We had a cat last year and a fox got it. The cat ran. Dad says if a cat sits still a fox won't touch it, only if it runs."

Caroline sat puzzling this.

"I hate foxes," said Shirley.

Neal had closed the door again.

"Wouldn't the dogs chase him?" Martin asked.

"Sure! And then we'd have them hollerin' up and down the hill all night, keeping you all awake. I'll put them out on the chain before we go to bed. If they git off by themselves, huntin', this time of year, they'll be gone for days."

"Isn't that the kind you hunt?"

"I get one once in a while. But their skin isn't worth much. Not like a good red fox."

"I remember one fall," Jimmie said, "there were a lot of them used to hang round in the hollow back there, and one time I went out to the spring after dark and I was coming back with the flashlight and there was a gray fox tracked me all the way back to the house. He kept a-hollerin', and I'd turn the flashlight on him and he'd run, and then he'd keep a-comin' again, and I got so mad I threw the flashlight right at him and I had to run home in the dark."

"Did you say 'mad,' Jim," inquired his father, winking at Martin, "or did you say 'scared'?"

"I said mad. I wasn't scared. I knew it was just a gray fox, all right, but any time I hear one of them darn things holler it makes me jump, and it would anyone else, too!"

"How big is a gray fox?" Caroline wanted to know.

"Not as big as you are, Sis!" and Caroline looked relieved. "They're about so long—" Neal spread his hands apart. "They're heavier built than a red fox, and sort of low in the body; a red fox is most all fur."

"Is there anything bigger than foxes?"

"There's wild cats. There was a lot of 'em round where I lived once. And there used to be a thing they called bobcats; some folks call it a link."

Martin nodded. "I've seen lynxes, in the zoo. They've got tufted ears."

"That was up among the big ledges, the place they call the Cat Rocks still, though I guess there's nothing much but snakes there now, up over west of here. I don't suppose there's been one of those things seen in years," Neal said.

"There used to be bears," Jimmie said. "Dad saw a bear once."

"I was always sure it was a bear, but when I told them at home no one believed me. You know how it is; if Jimmie were to come home one day and tell me he'd seen a tiger I'd just say, 'Yeah?' and think no more about it. Though they should have had more sense, for in my grandfather's day there used to be bears, back round the swamp there. I was going to school across lots by the short cut—just about Shirley's size, I was—and all at once I seen it standing up there in a berry patch, and I turned right around quick and came home. 'I ain't goin'

to school today,' I says, but when I told them all I got
was a licking. But I went back and found its tracks next
day, right along the brook where the ground was soft.
Just like a naked foot print. It was a bear, all right. I
can see it now, standing there. Of course if it was Jimmie,
now, he'd have walked right up to it and made sure!"

"I would not! Not without I had a gun with me."

"A gun wouldn't do you any good," said Martin.
"Father knew a man who met a bear right on a narrow
ledge of rock and he didn't have any weapon—he was
coming back from fishing—so he just waved his arms
and yelled and the bear ran away. He said he was glad
he didn't have a gun, 'cause he might have fired it, and
then the bear would have gone for him. It was up near
Canada. They had mountain lions there, too; panthers.
I guess there wouldn't be any panthers round here?"

"I wouldn't like to say there was. But there was a
queer thing happened when I was a boy," Neal said.
"I've often wondered about it. It was when we were living up in that house I showed you, the time we drove over
to the cider mill. The big swamp's right in back and it
used to be pretty wild up in there those days; not much
cleared land around. I'd gone over to my aunt's one day,
and I had my brother with me; he was just a bit younger
than Jimmie is now. It was getting on dusk and we was
coming back by the old corduroy road, not hurryin' any,

and all at once I heard something hollering up the hill
back of the swamp, a kind of a long howl: ooh—ooh—
ooh!

"I says: 'Hear that owl, Nate?' And Nate he looked
over his shoulder, sort of quick, and then he looked up at
me, but he didn't say nothing, so I says: 'Getting latish;
we'd better walk a bit faster!' I knew mighty well that
wasn't no owl we heard, and it wasn't a wildcat, either,
for I'd heard them screeching at night, and I knew what
they sounded like. This was bigger and deeper, and it
didn't sound like nothing I'd ever heard before; it was
a kind of a hunting cry, if you know what I mean.

"I didn't want to say nothing, for I didn't want to
get Nate scared, so we just kept right on going, walking
as fast as we could, and all the time I could feel him
pressin' up close to me, and then bye-an'-bye we heard it
again, a lot nearer this time: Ooh—oo—ooh!

"Then Nate looked at me, an' I looked at him, and
I says: 'Nate, *suppose we run?*' And he grabbed my hand
and we started to beat it, quick as we could, and as we
ran I heard the holler again, and this time I could tell by
the sound it was there on the corduroy road right back
of us. It was dark by then in under the trees and I never
run so fast in all my life, just dragging the kid along with
me, and pretty soon we were near the end of the road.
Our own house was quite a ways off still and there was

another long piece of woods to pass before we come to it, but there was another house nearer and I figured if we could make that and the folks were up still, we'd go in there and wait for a while before we went on home. So I says: 'Nate, if you can keep it up till we get to Johnson's we'll go in there, and if they're asleep we'll wake 'em up.'

"Well, when we got as far as the house there I felt pretty safe. All the folks were in bed—they kept pretty early hours as a rule—and the lights were all out. We crept up close under the front stoop and I said: 'Nate, I tell you what we'll do. We'll just wait here and listen till we hear it holler again, and then we'll know for sure which way it's headin', and if it's headin' this way we'll bang on the door till the folks come down and let us in.' For I hated to wake everyone up if we didn't have to, and I knew anyway we could get into the barn or somewheres at a pinch. So we waited, and we listened, and bye-an'-bye sure enough we did hear it. But it wasn't coming our way any more; either something had scared it or it was tracking something else, for it had turned off and was traveling down the valley. But my knees were still shaking, and so were Nate's, and we hung round that house quite a bit before we dared start on for home."

ACROSS THE ROAD

"Did you ever find out what it was?" Martin asked.

"No, I never did. But I know that about that time, or maybe a year or so later, there was two or three people had tales of seeing some big light-colored thing in the woods, different times, and all more or less around the same place. One was a peddler driving home at night, and he saw it, but it made off before he had a chance to see what it was. No one ever did know. But that swamp there joins right up with the woods in back and there's miles and miles of country out that way used to be pretty wild, and still is. And I've figured since that if some big animal ever did get down there from the forests up north it might live around there for years on what it could hunt, deer and things, without a soul ever setting eyes on it except by chance. I could show you places within fifteen miles of right here where we're sitting that's as wild as anything you find up north."

"You're going to have all these kids good and scared first thing you know," Mary put in. "That was years ago. If you heard anything howling these days it wouldn't be anything worse than a fox, like we heard tonight."

"Well, the land around here hasn't been farmed, not like it used to be, for quite a while now. People come here and buy up the big places and just keep them the way they are, for summer places or hunting and fishing clubs. The land's lapsing back to forest in lots of places, and first thing you know the wild things start coming back too."

It was later than usual when Martin and Caroline got their coats and said goodnight. Listening to Neal's story they had forgotten the clock, and Shirley was already half asleep in the sofa corner.

"Want me to walk across the road with you?" Neal asked as they stood in the doorway.

Had it been any other evening Martin might have said yes, but tonight pride prevented him. He wouldn't even take the flashlight Jimmie offered. It was his boast, especially before Caroline, that he never minded the dark.

"Well, I'll leave the door open awhile, so you can see your way down the path," Neal said.

Home was, if not exactly across the road, only a hundred yards up the road and then along the little pathway from the bars to the house. By daytime it was only a step, but at night even familiar distances have a curious and uncomfortable way of lengthening themselves out. When Martin and Caroline once left that comforting lane of yellow light flung from the Rowes' doorway they seemed to step at once into unfathomable blackness. Martin had a queer light feeling in his feet. Even the ground felt strange; the road rose up to meet one unexpectedly and then fell away, and the bushes and rocks all seemed to be in the wrong places. Nor did it help matters that Caroline had a tendency to clutch and stumble against him.

"Look out—what you want to go treading on my feet like that for!" he snapped, but his voice was a whisper. "Leggo, can't you?"

"It's—*dark!*" Caroline whimpered. "I can't see where I'm going!"

"Then hold my hand and walk where I tell you."

"I'm scared of the fox."

"Don't be so silly! Foxes don't hurt you. That fox went off ages ago; he's way up the hill by now."

Never had home seemed so far away. For a moment Martin almost felt himself in Neal's shoes, years ago; he thought he knew now just how Neal must have felt on that old corduroy road. Suppose it were true that big things did come down, sometimes, still, from the forests? And the swamp was not so very far away, after all.

It was certainly a mercy that the gray fox did not choose that particular moment to "holler" again, as Neal called it. As it was, a rustling in the dead roadside bushes ahead of them brought Martin to a sharp standstill, his heart pounding, while Caroline let out a strangled squeal. But it was only Garry, groping her way towards them.

"It's so dark I thought I'd come out and meet you; I

saw the door open. You must have been there for hours!"

Caroline clung to her, as she had clung a moment ago to Martin but with far greater confidence. With Garry around nothing could happen.

"Garry, did you hear the fox?"

"I heard something a while back; sounded like a cat fight."

The road was familiar again. Light showed faintly through the chinks where Kay had drawn the curtains.

"Look out for the rock there, Caroline; here's where the path turns in. Not a star out! Wasn't it pretty black coming up the hill there?"

"Not so bad. It's only a step, anyway," said Martin.

Next morning there was a queer stillness outside the little house, and it seemed lighter than usual. Martin, first to wake, stumbled to his window and pulled aside the shade. Field and hillside lay smooth and white, blanketed under a three-inch snowfall.

☆　　✮　　**IV**　　✮　　☆

The Boll Weevil

"TWO letters for Kay, one for you, Penny, and the newspaper," Garry announced, stamping the snow off her feet as she came in from the mailbox. "Why I never get any mail in this household I don't know. I shall start writing letters to myself soon."

She knew the writing on one of the envelopes she dropped into Kay's lap and smiled as she slipped it uppermost.

"Nothing from father?" said Mrs. Ellis. "Well, he never does write often."

"It's only ten days," Garry reminded her. "If father writes once in three weeks he's doing wonders. The best way is for us to miss writing to him, once in a while."

Her mother read through her letter slowly and then sat for a moment holding the thin close-written pages on her knee, her face troubled.

"Nothing wrong with Aunt Margaret?"

"No, she's all right. Peggy isn't very well. She was a long time getting over that flu, and now the doctor says she has a spot on her lung and he wants her to go straight off to New Mexico for the winter."

"Tough luck. Poor Peggy! Is she very bad?" Garry asked, while Kay looked up from her letter.

"No, he thinks the winter out there should put it right. But she has to be pretty careful. The trouble for Aunt Margaret is that she can't possibly go down there with her now that she has this job and Peggy can't go alone; there's got to be someone to look after her. She wants to know if I could go; she says she would rather have me than anyone because she'll feel so much easier if I'm there, but I don't see . . ."

"Could I be any use?" asked Kay quickly.

"My dear, I'd propose it in a minute, but you know how Aunt Margaret is, and you know what Peggy is like. It's got to be some older person who can keep her in order and make her mind. You're both too much of an age for you to have any sort of control over her, and it isn't even as if she were actually ill and had to stay in bed. It was through all this racketing around and late hours that she got sick in the first place, and I imagine that's one reason why the doctor wants to get her right out of town. No, Kay, I wish you could, for it would be a grand chance for you and perhaps later Aunt Margaret would be glad of it, but you'd be no use just now. And I can't think of anybody else."

"Of course you can go," said Garry promptly. "We can get along here perfectly well by ourselves and it would do you a whole lot of good, too. How long is it for?"

"Aunt Margaret thought for a month or so anyway, till she could make some other arrangement. She really is at her wit's end, this happening just now. She says she insists on making it a business arrangement; someone would have to go anyway, and Peggy's uncle is helping with the expenses."

"Then that settles it. The idea of an Ellis turning down a job, and in New Mexico at that! I call it a rank piece of luck," Garry decided.

"It wouldn't be much, I imagine, but at least it would pay for someone to stay here with you while I'm away, and I shall have practically no expenses myself to think of. I do hate to refuse if it can be managed, for Aunt Margaret has always been so good to us and this would be a chance to help her out in return." Mrs. Ellis's face cleared as she spoke.

"Yes, when I think of relations I never count Aunt Margaret in with them. She's quite different," Garry agreed.

"We won't need anyone," Kay said. "Garry and I can

[65]

manage perfectly and you won't have to worry about the children, for one of us will write to you every two days. And there are the Rowes right across the way. It isn't a bit like being alone here."

"Yes, I'm glad of that; we couldn't have kinder neighbors. But there has got to be someone in the house; I wouldn't dream of it otherwise, in winter and all."

"I don't suppose it'll be any worse winter than it is now," Garry said, "and anyway someone else in the house isn't going to prevent it. What we will do before you go is to have a telephone put in; then we can always call up if we need to without going across the road in bad weather, and you'll feel safer about us. That's much more important. Now you write your wire to Aunt Margaret so as to set her mind at rest and I'll take it right over to Mary's, and then we can talk about the rest."

Garry had a way of clinching matters.

The telephone was put in; hitherto they had managed without it, for the two houses were so near it was very little trouble to slip across. But about the "someone" Mrs. Ellis was firm. Edna would have been the real person but Edna couldn't leave home, and there was no one else in the neighborhood. In the end, and reluctantly, Cousin Carrie was appealed to, after much groaning from Kay and Garry. Cousin Carrie was interested in various kinds of social work and could generally be relied upon to "know of someone" among her many protégés. She knew of someone now.

"It is difficult," she wrote, "to find exactly the type of person you want at such short notice, for most of the women I know who are out of jobs and might be glad of such an opportunity are far too young. I think I have been fortunate therefore in getting hold of Mrs. Cummings. She has been living with a married daughter recently but before that worked as housekeeper and caretaker for several good families. She is used to the country and thoroughly reliable, elderly but quite capable of light assistance and general supervision, and with two grown girls in the house that is all that should be necessary. She would be willing to come to you for forty dollars a month and her keep, but I gather that under the circumstances would expect to be treated as one of the family."

"What else would one expect?" commented Garry when the letter was read aloud. "We're plain people; no room here for a servants' hall if we wanted one. But I think if she's only going to give light assistance and be treated as one of the family forty dollars is a lot of money these days. I'd expect to *work* for forty dollars a month."

Mrs. Ellis privately thought so too, for forty dollars all but swallowed up the little sum that her sister would be able to pay her and she had hoped to be able to send something home as well, for little extra comforts. But Cousin Carrie evidently knew, and there was no time to pick and choose, as she reminded herself; the main thing was to have someone responsible in the house.

"What does she mean by 'general supervision'?" Kay wondered. "She isn't going to be in charge of us, anyway."

"It's Cousin Carrie's delicate way of suggesting a chaperone," Garry explained. "Obsolete term, to be found in all good Victorian dictionaries. Look it up, Kay."

"Don't be absurd," said her mother. "Cousin Carrie just means that she's capable and responsible. She's probably just some nice middle-aged person who will be glad of a good home and a little change."

"She'll probably get the little change, all right," Garry said. "I don't know so much about the pleasant home. Don't look that way, Penny dear! You know we are perfect models always when you aren't around to set a bad example. I expect she'll teach me knitting stitches of an evening while Kay reads the paper aloud."

Penny was to leave as soon as possible, so the next few days were busy ones. Martin was frankly envious of anyone going to New Mexico; it was just the sort of thing that would happen to a girl and not a boy, who would have known how to appreciate it. He had no sympathy at all for Peggy, and thought her plain lucky. Kay felt secretly a little the same way. She was glad for her mother to have the change and experience but would have given a great deal to be in her shoes, for Santa Fé called up visions of everything she would most have loved, sunlight and color and a world of new impressions, and most likely the chance of meeting painters and writers as well. A great deal of longing and some bitterness of feeling—not for her mother but with life in general—was packed into the suitcase along with the rolled stockings and underwear. Things always happened, she thought, to people who didn't particularly want them at the moment, never to those who did.

Caroline took the upheaval calmly, as she did most things. Her own small life always went on steadily in the middle of whatever might be whirling about her. But one never knew just what special detail would take root in Caroline's mind, to be brooded over quietly, and Garry, coming into the tiny alcove room one night to tuck her up, found her sitting up in bed with a deep and thoughtful expression.

"Garry, what is a spot on your lung?"

Garry thought a moment.

"It's when you've had a bad cold and haven't taken care of it or something, and it gets down in your lungs and

[69]

starts trouble, and then if you aren't careful you get t.b."

"Do you suppose I could have got a spot on my lungs?"

"I don't think it's at all likely."

"Then what," asked Caroline dramatically, "would you say this is!" And she pulled her flannelette night-gown open, exposing a small red dot on her firm chest.

"That," said Garry, moving the candle so as to examine it attentively, "is probably a last summer's mosquito bite."

"But it's right where my lungs are, and I've had it for months. It doesn't ever go away." Caroline's voice sounded sepulchral.

"That's because you keep on scratching it," said her sister, dashing all Caroline's carefully built dreams of importance to the ground at one unfeeling blow. "Now shut your eyes and go to sleep."

It seemed only a day between Aunt Margaret's letter and the final moment when Edna drew up at the house, cheery as usual.

"Just you have a good time and don't you worry about the family, Mrs. Ellis," she said, while Garry and Martin were hoisting suitcases into the back of the car. "I'll drive out once in a while to keep an eye on them. I'd take the whole bunch down to the station now only I've got another job and I wouldn't be able to get them back in the time. Here, I brought a cushion to tuck in back of you. This road's awful bouncy now the ruts are all frozen up."

And Mary Rowe came flying across the road, bare-headed as usual.

"Good-bye, and you remember Neal and I are right across the way here. If the chimney burns down or the weather gets too cold they can all come over and live with us. There's plenty of room. I mean it. Jimmie wants you to mail him a horned toad from New Mexico if you find one, but I told him you'd be far too busy. And I hope the niece gets well soon!"

"I don't suppose it will be for more than a few weeks," Mrs. Ellis said as they crowded round for the last hug. "I expect Aunt Margaret herself may be able to come down there later, or someone else will. Take good care of yourself and write to me every week!"

Then the car was off, growing smaller and smaller as it jolted down the hill. Mary promptly took Caroline back with her to bake cookies with Shirley; Martin went off whistling a little louder than usual to hide his feelings; and the two girls were left to the sympathy of Mrs. Cummings, hovering with a helpful air in the background.

Mrs. Cummings had arrived the day before. Edna drove her up from the station, and Edna's face was a study as she helped the old lady out. Mrs. Cummings was smiling and voluble and what Garry called "mousey." She was sure, before she had been ten minutes in the house, that everything was "very nice," and that she and the dear girls—an expression which enraged Kay from the start—were going to get along very nicely, very nicely indeed. And they mustn't bother about her or put themselves out in any way, she could make herself comfortable anywhere.

They had arranged for her the little parlor off the living room, which had a fireplace, and which with a little change of furnishings made a very pleasant bedroom. Here, with her trunk and suitcase, she was left to unpack before supper, expressing great contentment that everything was so nice, although Kay, happening to glance back as she left the room, saw her scuttle noiselessly to the bedside and turn up a corner of the mattress to see what it was made of.

On the whole she seemed, as Mrs. Ellis tried to think after a short interview, a pleasant and homely sort of person who would fit without too much difficulty into the household.

But if anything could have made Kay and Garry more homesick in those first few days after their mother left, it was Mrs. Cummings's presence. Home alone, even empty as it seemed, would not have been so bad, but complicated by a stranger's presence it was dreadful. Especially one, who, like Mrs. Cummings, seemed to pervade the whole household.

Whatever they might think of Cousin Carrie's choice, the two girls did their best to make the old lady feel comfortable and at home. With an instinctive sense of how they themselves might feel under similar circumstances in a strange household, they tried to treat her as they would any other middle-aged guest, on a friendly footing, with the inevitable result that Mrs. Cummings became, before very long, rather like the cuckoo in the sparrows' nest.

Her possessions, and she had a surprising number of them, began to spill over from her own room. Kay, who was perhaps a little exaggerated about orderliness and always tried to keep the house looking its best, had to get used to seeing the old lady's spectacles, her shawl, her crochet, the sweater she thought she would wear and afterwards took off, the newspaper she thought she was going to read later on, left lying about the living room, or worse, bestowed in certain nooks and receptacles which Mrs. Cummings had adopted, squirrel-like, for her own; one being Kay's pet Chinese bowl on the cupboard top, another the mantelpiece, which Kay liked to keep in a certain studied arrangement and which the old lady thought particularly adapted for keeping minor articles she was liable to mislay and wanted in full sight. There was only one really good lamp in the living room, and this Mrs. Cummings managed firmly to arrange in such a position on the table that it threw plenty of light on the comfortable armchair she occupied near the stove, and none at all anywhere else.

"I told you she was mousey," said Garry after a few days.

In the kitchen it was just as bad. She wanted everything arranged in a different way.

"Don't you think it would be handier if we kept the cups and saucers here and the bread box there?"

"Don't you think it would be handier if the oranges went into the pantry instead of that blue bowl, and then we'd have the chest free to stack dishes on?"

"Don't you think . . ."

Garry, who with Martin's help looked after the few outdoor chores, had her own troubles. She had always kept the wood-box filled and the stoves attended to, but as early as three o'clock Mrs. Cummings would begin to worry about whether the firewood was going to last through the evening or whether it wasn't. And then it would be: "Don't you think, while it's still nice and light . . ."

"Take my advice," said that young woman one morning, sternly setting the blue bowl of oranges back where it had always been kept. "If you let her get one triumph—just one—we'll be done for."

Nevertheless and imperceptibly the household began to find itself organized according to Mrs. Cummings's ideas of comfort. Not that she did very much herself, after the first week, except sit around and keep warm, but she loved to suggest, and Cousin Carrie's reference to general supervision became only too clear. Meal hours were changed about. Mrs. Cummings ate no breakfast, so she usually began to feel faintish about noon, and supper was an hour earlier so that things could be "got out of the way." Getting things out of the way and having things "handy," though apparently contradictory terms, were among her firm beliefs. Worst of all, she referred to the absent Penny frequently and invariably as "your dear Ma."

Caroline was the one who got along with her best. Over Caroline she seemed to exert a peculiar fascination. Caroline would follow her about, watching her, or with the small girl's insatiable interest in the conversation of elder persons, sit spellbound listening to Mrs. Cummings's accounts of the various places she had lived in, all of them, it began gradually to appear, superior in every detail to the Ellis household.

"*You're* an old-fashioned one!" Mrs. Cummings would remark to her occasionally. Caroline seemed to take it as a compliment.

More and more often Kay and Garry, as well as the younger ones, took to slipping over to the Rowes.

"What did she come for if she can't even get the supper by herself once in a while?" Mary asked bluntly one afternoon when Kay explained that she had to hurry home.

"It isn't that so much," Kay said. "Garry and I don't mind doing things; we always have. Only it's worse than having no one in the house at all. And nothing's ever quite right, though goodness knows we've turned the place upside down to make her comfortable. She says her room's like an ice box, though she's got every extra quilt in the house on her bed this minute, with the fireplace as well, and Garry and I were freezing last night. She didn't seem a bit like that when she first came, but I suppose you never do know how people will turn out."

"I tell you, you want to *watch* her," said Mary, who had paid more than one visit to the Ellis house. "She reminds me of nothing in the world so much as the boll weevil in that Carl Sandburg record!"

"You can't tell me a thing about old ladies," said Edna, who had faithfully driven over one day to see how the family were getting along, and in two minutes had shrewdly summed up the situation. "I've had plenty to do with them and I know." And noticing Kay's worried face and Garry's curt cheerfulness she added sensibly: "You'd better all of you pile right in my car this minute and we'll go down to town to see the movies. I've got a free evening and the roads are fine, and I'll get you back before bedtime."

The movies—even those that the one local picture house afforded in this off season—followed by hot chocolate at the corner drugstore, seemed like positive dissipation after so many shut-in weeks on the hillside. It was cheerful to see lights and shop windows and people walking about on sidewalks again, and the drive home over frozen roads and under a clear star-lighted sky, singing at the tops of their voices while Edna steered skilfully between the bumps, was almost the best part of the evening. They returned blessing Edna, and with renewed strength to cope with Mrs. Cummings through another week at least.

Neal referred to her cheerfully as "the old gal." "How's your old gal getting along?" he would ask the girls whenever he saw them.

"You see, you didn't start right," he told them one day. "What you ought to have done was just to have

WINTERBOUND

buttered her feet a bit, see, like they do to cats in a strange
place. Then she'd have been kept so busy lickin' the butter off she wouldn't have no time for complaints."

"Seems to me we've done nothing but butter her feet,
ever since she came in the house," said Garry, "and that's
the whole trouble."

"Well, we had a little heart to heart talk, out here on
the road the other day," Neal went on. "She told me how
terrible everything was in the country, and I told *her* how
terrible everything was in the country, and believe me I
could tell her a whole lot more'n she could tell me. I just
jollied her along and she took it all like a lamb, and I
could see she was getting the impression I was a nice,
quiet, intelligent sort of a guy, someone she felt she could
have real confidence in. I tell you, what that old soul
needs is just to forget her troubles and get out and have a
good time for once. Some night I'm going to shave real
well and get my best pants on and take her out to one of
these country dances over at Warley Center or some
place. You see if I don't!"

But for all Neal's joking things went from bad to
worse.

The brunt of it fell upon Kay, for Garry could always
basely find some excuse for outdoor jobs, preferring the
biting cold to Mrs. Cummings's running monologues.
The absence of a radio was one grievance; she'd have

[78]

thought everyone had a radio, these days. But there were plenty of others. It was not pleasant to be reminded continually, in not too roundabout a way, how much better built, better equipped, and better managed other people's houses were; how Mrs. Cummings's own daughter had a little house so snug, you wouldn't believe it, everything was so handy and kept like a new pin; her husband got her an electric egg beater only the other day. How all the other country places Mrs. Cummings had ever lived in before had electricity and furnaces and plumbing; running water upstairs and down, and everything so "nice." How Mrs. Cummings never could bear stoves, nasty dirty things with all the mess and ashes, and as for pumps—why, hardly anybody these days put up with a pump. So unhandy!

Well-to-do people, it seemed, were what Mrs. Cummings had always been used to. Her last place now, out on Long Island, she'd had her own bathroom with a shower in it, and everything so comfortable. Kay ought to see how people lived, nice people. She managed to convey that poverty, even temporary, was rather a disgrace and that not having certain luxuries stamped one, as it were. Mrs. Sterling had a lovely apartment; she'd often gone there to help with sewing or spring cleaning, and she'd do anything to oblige Mrs. Sterling who was such a nice lady, but if she'd known the sort of place she was coming to—well, there! It couldn't be helped, so the only thing was to make the best of it.

Even the goaded worm will turn at last and Kay, one morning when the pump had frozen unexpectedly, Big Bertha for some reason refused to draw, and Caroline in the general confusion had forgotten to put on her heavy sweater under her school coat and the omission was only found out too late to remedy, turned upon Mrs. Cummings in exasperation.

"If you were so comfortable at your daughter's house, Mrs. Cummings, and you really feel that way about everything, I should think you'd better go back there," she said.

Garry, still tinkering with the pump and a kettle of boiling water in the back kitchen, could hardly believe her ears. It was very seldom that Kay lost her temper, but this was one of the times. Garry recognized that tone, not so very different from Penny's when Penny got thoroughly mad.

One retort led to another; there was a sharp brief battle of words from which Kay emerged shaken but victorious, with an odd sensation of feeling herself for the first time head of the household in her mother's absence. Mrs. Cummings retired to her room; lunch, when it came, was a silent and extra-polite meal and later Garry whispered over the dishpan:

THE BOLL WEEVIL

"Do you suppose she's really going?"

"She's been acting for days as if she wanted to, and I told her she could. She's probably packing her trunk now. Garry, I just couldn't have stood another single day of it!"

"I know it, old girl. I'm darn glad you spoke out. Home will be home again, anyway!"

"Mother will be worried, I suppose, and Cousin Carrie furious when she hears, but I just don't care. We can always get someone else if we have to."

"No more of Cousin Carrie's old bats, thank you. Why, Penny would never have stood her a day, I know! To think of all the women out of jobs who'd have been glad to come here if they only knew, and could have a good time with us." Garry swished the milk pitcher out vigorously.

"Oh, I don't suppose this place is such a catch! It is uncomfortable and muddly and hard work in winter, but it's no better for being told about it every minute of the day."

When Mrs. Cummings emerged, closing the door carefully behind her, it was to call up the station for a taxi, disdaining Edna. But there was only one train a day in winter—Garry could have told her that much—so another uncomfortable twenty-fours hours had still to pass. Mrs. Cummings improved them by being unusually nice to Caroline, managing to treat her with an air of veiled pity. Her silence towards the rest of the family seemed to denote a meek acceptance rather unexpected in her, but Kay was to find a surprise still in store.

"The month is not up for three days yet, Mrs. Cummings, and mother paid you that before she left, so I don't think we owe each other anything," said Kay next morning, feeling a little uncomfortable now the storm was over and hoping for at least a pleasant leave-taking.

"There's next month's salary due to me, Miss Ellis," returned the old lady, having sized up Kay's inexperience long ago.

"*Next* month?"

"A month's pay or a month's notice, that's always understood, Miss Ellis. It was you that give the notice, not me. The arrangement as I understood it was for two months at least, and there's my fares and expenses to be thought of, not to speak of my having thrown over another very good job just to come up here to you, on account of obliging Mrs. Sterling and all, though what I'm to say to her . . ."

"You needn't trouble about Mrs. Sterling," said Kay, white with anger. "I shall tell her myself everything that is necessary. And I think it will be a very long time before she finds you another place!"

Garry, always the level-headed one, was not there

at the moment to consult, there was no time to run over and ask Mary about it, and Kay marched upstairs to the little box that held the store of housekeeping money her mother had left, took out four bills, and coming back laid them silently on the table.

She was too angry to mention the matter until after the taxi had driven away, and then she told Garry, who whistled.

"Good Lord, Kay! But she'd no right to it at all!"

"I don't know, she said she had, and I was just too mad at the whole business to argue with her. I'd rather give her the forty dollars and have done with it, though I suppose I was a fool and I don't believe one word about that other job she missed taking. We'd have paid it anyhow if she had stayed on."

"Well, depend upon it she'll take good care to steer clear of Cousin Carrie for a while now, anyway, which is something to be thankful for. So Cousin Carrie won't know a thing and we needn't have to worry mother about it all. Cheer up, Kay! We've got the house to ourselves again, and it's only three days to Christmas!"

Mary Rowe's comment was brief and pointed.

"The old buzzard!" she exclaimed when Garry told her. "To think of getting away with forty dollars like that! Well, if you ask me I don't know but it's cheap at the price."

WINTERBOUND

All the same the living room, denuded of Mrs. Cummings's familiar flotsam and jetsam, had an oddly empty look that evening, and Kay and Garry found themselves wondering if after all they had done everything they could to make the old lady's stay comfortable, and whether they mightn't have shown a little more patience with her ways—the sort of uncomfortable regret that always attends the departure of people one has disliked but never of those one cares for. Still, as Garry said, it was only three more days to Christmas.

Ways and Means

CHRISTMAS day dawned clear and fine; a white Christmas, for there had been a fresh fall of snow overnight. There was no wind, so trees and bushes held their delicate white tracery on every twig, and the dead weeds by the gateway were changed suddenly to things of beauty.

For days past the children had been busily concealing secrets from each other and from their elders. What Christmas shopping there was—for the younger ones only—had been done long ago through the mail-order catalogue and had duly arrived and been secreted. Yesterday's mail had been a heavy and exciting one; even the usually grumpy mailman had a smile for Caroline as she waited by the box. There were thick letters from father and mother among the rest, Christmas cards and several gayly tagged parcels, to be opened on Christmas morning.

One from mother and Peggy, with a slender silver-and-turquoise chain for Kay, an odd little Indian bowl for Garry, a pocket folder of Indian leather work for Martin, and a tiny silver ring shaped like a snake with a turquoise in his head, that just fitted Caroline's middle finger.

"I wish we could have sent her something," Kay said as they unpacked the box.

"Your cards were lovely, Kay; she and father would rather have had those than anything, and she'll have got Caroline's kettle holder by now, though goodness knows what she'll have to use it on, out there."

"I guess they make tea in New Mexico," said Caroline, studying the effect of the blue ring on her pink finger.

"There'll be tea made anywhere where Penny is," Garry assured her, quick to make amends. "She can always find use for a kettle holder if it's only to pick things up outdoors when the sun is too hot, and if your penwiper doesn't reach father quite by Christmas he'll have it for New Year's anyway, and that's just as good. Now hurry up and open the rest!"

Candy from Aunt Margaret and another box of candy for Kay, with no name. Silk stockings, handkerchiefs for Caroline, and a tie for Martin. More stockings and socks, green ski pants for Caroline, an embroidered handkerchief case that must have come from one of Cousin Carrie's bazaars, a diary, three woolen mufflers and a pretty brown sweater—the relatives had gone in heavily for clothing this year—a white china monkey with glass eyes and a hole in his back to put flowers in, a bottle of bath salts, and a rabbit made of green soap and clad in a pink washcloth.

"Someone must think we don't take enough baths," Kay laughed.

"They're probably right, but just try it this weather, with a tin bathtub in a drafty kitchen! I wish we'd had the bath salts earlier; they might have impressed Mrs. Cummings, anyway," said Garry. "Now let's see. One of these boxes of candy will go to the Rowes; that's fine. Don't collapse, Martin; we'll all be there to eat it just the same. We'll give Neal my diary. It's swell and useful, but I'd just as soon have one from the ten-cent store next time Edna goes there. Do we need three mufflers in the family?"

"One would be nice for Mary, but I'd rather give her this sweater," Kay decided. "It's so pretty and my others are still perfectly good, and I know she'd use this more than she would a muffler."

"Grand," said Garry with an extra warmth of tone, for she knew that Kay's sweaters were far from perfectly good, having seen more than one season's wear already. "Then the extra muffler will do for Jimmie. Get me that roll of red paper in the table drawer, Caroline, and see if you can smooth some of this ribbon out."

[87]

WINTERBOUND

The room looked Christmas-like with green boughs above the mantelpiece and trailing ground pine in the Chinese bowl. Two days ago Neal had chosen and cut the two little trees, one for each family, taking the children with him on this annual excursion up the hillside, and Kay had trimmed their own from the box of Christmas-tree "orderments," as Caroline used to call them, saved and put by from year to year and which they had remembered to bring with them even though the packing and moving took place in June. So all the familiar colored balls and dangles and shining gold and silver fruits hung there—or at least as many as the tree would hold—and the waxen Christmas angel, a bit smudgy from repeated handling, smiled from the top branch and the pink spun-glass bird chirped silently just below him, as they had done for so many Christmases before in different surroundings.

"The Christmas angel's got a regular grin on him," Martin said, reaching to straighten the old friend, who having lost half a wing soared rather lopsidedly.

"I should think he would," returned Garry. "There! I think those look all right."

She surveyed the parcels. No one could really tell, unless they looked hard, that the holly-printed ribbon had been twice used. Christmas dinner was to be at the Rowes, but not till two o'clock, for every Christmas Day

Neal went out fox hunting; it was the one date in the year, he said, that he never failed to keep, so the family dinner was put off till his return.

The children spent the morning coasting, not on the road, which was steep and dangerous and forbidden except in the company of elder people, but on the pasture slope behind the Rowes' barn, where the occasional rocks and bumps were just enough to make the run exciting. Caroline had her new ski pants on, long, warm, and full around the ankles above her arctics, and Shirley had a pair, too, brown ones. Caroline's had come from a New York store and Shirley's from the faithful mail-order catalogue, but the children decided there was little to choose between them. Wading through the snow, dragging the sled behind them, the little girls looked like two long-legged gnomes, one brown, one green.

Kay and Garry were just setting out for the house when Neal returned, old black-and-tan Sam at his heels. He had his gun over one shoulder, something limp and soft and tawny slung across the other, which he dropped on the snow at their feet.

"Merry Christmas! How's that for a nice fox?"

"Merry Christmas! Not such a merry Christmas for the fox though," returned Garry quickly, for she hated to see anything dead and that clean shining fur, the still slim paws and pointed nose gave her a pang of regret for

WINTERBOUND

what had been only a little while ago a living flash of
speed and pride and beauty. But Neal was so cheerful
and pleased about it; a fox skin she knew was worth ten
dollars and ten dollars meant a good deal to the Rowe
family. "It's a beauty, Neal! Where did you get it?"

"Up over Crooked Hill. He cost me three hours tracking and a six-mile walk. Well, old Sam and me decided
we wouldn't come home without we'd earned our dinner,
and I guess we have."

"What does he weigh?" Martin asked. The younger
ones had gathered eagerly round.

"Not what you'd think. A bit more than a good-sized
cat. Mostly all fur, you see; that's what makes them hard
to hit. Lot's of times you think you've hit a fox, and all
you hit is his fur."

"It looks like a dog," Caroline said. But as she drew
nearer there was something not at all like a dog in the
slant of the half-closed eyes, the warning lift of the lip
above white shining teeth; that subtle difference which
always sets apart the wild thing from the tame one, even
in death. Not a nice thing to meet, Caroline thought, and
remembered the gray fox that had howled behind the
barn.

"Want to try a fine warm neckpiece, Caroline?"

But Caroline shrank back as Neal lifted the dead fox
to his shoulder.

[90]

WAYS AND MEANS

Mary was waiting for them in the doorway. There was a grand smell of roast goose and mince pie, apple sauce and baking sweet potatoes as they crowded into the kitchen where the big table was already set. A happy joking meal, with the box of candy to finish up with and a bottle of Mary's special three-year-old dandelion wine to drink a toast to the absent ones.

"What I call a dinner!" said Jimmie.

"Two Christmases ago," Neal said, "I'd been out of work for quite a spell and we were sitting down round this table here to a nice dish of frankfurters and boiled potatoes. I don't know how come we happened to get the frankfurters, either, but anyway all at once there was a sort of crash outside, right against the woodshed door, and old Sam he started up and near knocked the table over. I went to open the door, and there outside was standing the prettiest two-year-old buck I ever saw, right there in the yard. Some dogs must have been chasing him and he'd come running down the hill, scared nearly to death, and turned right into the dooryard not knowing which way to go. I looked at him, and he looked at me, and then he got his breath and started off again down the pasture, and I said to Mary: 'Can you beat that! Here comes our Christmas dinner knocking right at the door, and we can't touch it!' "

"You can't shoot a deer any time?" asked Martin.

"Not any time, not until they make an open season again, and there hasn't been that in years. Only if it's on your own land and you can prove to the game warden they've been doing damage. I kind of hate to shoot a deer any time, law or no law, but that was one time I did feel sore about it. There he stood, and there was my gun right in the corner, and just frankfurters for Christmas!"

There was a log fire burning in the parlor and when the dishes were stacked the four older ones gathered there, while the little girls played house with the doll's bed and tiny table that Jimmie and Martin had made and painted and the new china tea set and shining pots and pans, and the boys went out again to coast by themselves. Mary brought out a hooked rug she had just started and a boxful of rags ready cut and wound into balls for working, and the sight of the soft faded colors set Kay off immediately on suggestions for design. While their two heads were bent over the hooking frame Garry and Neal played checkers by the fire and Tommy, who had been too excited by Christmas to take his usual nap, rolled and unrolled the colored balls all over the floor with the help of the youngest cat.

It was nearly dusk when they started home, and as Mary stood in the door with them she said: "I'm certainly going to miss you people if you ever go away. I hope you never do!"

WAYS AND MEANS

"If we do, we'll come back here every year for Christmas!"

Kay had been so fascinated watching the rug pattern grow under Mary's fingers that she wanted to start one for herself. Like everything that Kay began it was bound to be something ambitious and unusual. Trunks and closets were rummaged for old material that could be dyed, since very little of the Ellis's discarded wardrobe was of the colors she wanted. Mary had lent her an extra rugging hook, Neal made a frame, and she wrote off to Edna for dyes and burlap. Garry, who never minded staining her hands, mixed and boiled over the kitchen stove, and the insides of the family saucepans and kettles developed strange hues that refused to scour off. Things hung outdoors were frozen stiff this weather, so the woodshed was draped with lines of dripping color, and Garry's winter salad, if it ever sprouted at all, threatened to come up striped like Joseph's coat. Hooking was harder work than Kay realized; her fingertips grew sore tugging the rags through the stiff burlap, but she kept on at it doggedly, neglecting everything else.

Caroline had no part in these activities except to help in cutting up rags, of which she soon tired. The after-Christmas days began to weigh on her heavily. The boys were busy on their own affairs and Shirley was in bed with a cold. She took to hanging aimlessly about and one morning when the girls wanted to discuss something in peace and quiet Garry turned on her.

"Can't you for heaven's sake find something to *do,* Caroline! With this whole house and the state of Connecticut to play in, you've got to stick right under foot every minute. Now go—scat and vamoose. Beat it!"

"I'm going," Caroline ruffled like an angry chicken. "I was just going anyhow. And you needn't be so smart either and give yourself all those idiotic airs just because you think you look like Amelia Earhart with your hair that way, 'cause you don't, even if you do keep her picture stuck away in your bureau drawer to look at when you think nobody knows about it."

Garry made a feint with the dishcloth, for that particular shaft went home.

"That child gets worse and worse. I don't know what's come over her these days," declared Kay as the kitchen door slammed. "She doesn't get it from the Rowes, anyway."

"Did you ever hear Shirley when she gets thoroughly mad?" asked Garry, smiling in spite of herself. "Caroline needs Penny's stern hand; she's the only one to keep her in order."

"She'll get more than Penny's hand; she'll get mine, pretty quick, if she doesn't mend her ways. I do think little girls when they get that age are absolutely detestable," Kay seemed to forget that she had ever gone through that same detestable stage herself.

"Well, school begins Monday, praise be. Let's get back to this bill situation. How do we stand?"

"Nowhere." Kay bent a worried look on the pile of close-written grocery slips in her hand. "They all come in a bunch. I've paid the telephone and I thought I'd paid up the meat market, but now half of last month's things seem to have come on this. And there's the grocery. Garry, do *you* remember that we had four dozen eggs last month? We couldn't possibly. We were getting eggs from Mary right along."

"There was the time their hens stopped laying," Garry remembered. "Mary didn't have enough to give us. It must have been then."

"And butter. What we do with butter I don't know. Penny said to check our slips over every week and I always mean to, but I guess I haven't. We must have ordered an awful lot of stuff while the Cummings was here; she was forever telling me we were out of things and I just put them down without looking, I suppose. We did get some extra things over Christmas, and the meat bill's heavy because I feel with Martin and Caroline walking all that way to the bus every day they've got to have good meals when they come home. And then there's

[95]

their green vegetables, too. Caroline fusses over cabbage and I always thought spinach was cheap, but here it's been eighteen cents a pound all this time. And there were Martin's shoes. Those are extra, but that would only make three dollars off."

Garry studied the slips spread on the table, whistling softly.

"It does seem a lot, just for eating. What do you do—make the list just as you think?" For so far the house-keeping had been entirely in Kay's hands.

"I go through the pantry and order what we're out of and what I think we'll need. It's how Penny always did. I guess I'm so scared of running out of things that I get more than we really want, each time. It's all right only instead of spending less since Penny left we seem to be spending more," said Kay ruefully. "We're going to be awfully short this month when we get everything paid up and I hate to ask for more. She wrote us she had that dentist bill down there and I never told her I paid Mrs. Cummings that extra month. Those forty dollars would just put us right, now."

"I hope she chokes on them," said Garry, referring to Mrs. Cummings, not to Penny. "But if she did I suppose we wouldn't hear about it, so that's no comfort. I wish there was some way we could make money. The big idea

would be to make more, not to spend less. But I don't
suppose there's a thing." She gazed round the room.
"Rugs. But they take forever to hook, and then who's
going to buy them."

"All New England is full of hooked rugs. That's no
good. I did have an idea, but it never came to anything.
There was a man I met last spring and he saw some of
my work and liked it, and he thought maybe he could get
me some work illustrating. He knows some magazine
people and publishers, and he wanted to show them a few
drawings I had. I didn't hear anything for months and
months, and I was kind of hoping about it still, and then
he wrote me the other day." Kay paused. "He said they
liked them but it wasn't the kind of work they wanted,
and I didn't know enough about the way drawings have
to be made for reproduction. They all thought what I
needed was to take a year in illustrating class before I
could turn out anything they'd be able to use. He was
quite nice about it, and I guess he took quite a lot of
trouble, but there it is."

"Kay, what a darn shame! You never said a word
about it."

"There wasn't any good. I wouldn't have told you
now, only I hate to be just sitting round at home as if I
wasn't even trying to do anything."

"You *can* draw," said Garry hotly.

"I can draw, but I can't draw well enough. Oh, I know all that, but what does make me mad is people wanting to give you good advice and telling you all the things you know for yourself when they don't even understand your circumstances. I know well enough what I ought to be doing, but I just can't do it. I need to work and study and see things, and maybe go around and talk to publishers myself, and learn a whole lot I don't know, but you can't do all that from up here."

"Why can't you go to town for a while. I can look after things."

"It wouldn't be any use," Kay shook her head. "I've just got to wait, that's all. I don't know why I have to spill all this on you, except that I can't help getting sore sometimes when there's such a lot I want to do and no chance of doing it. I think everybody ought to be self-supporting by the time they're nineteen, and look at me!"

There was a tap at the door. Neal came in.

"Good morning. Did I break up the meeting?"

"Not a bit. We were just having a ways-and-means committee." Kay bundled the slips back into the table drawer.

"You're lucky, at that," Neal grinned. "We can't even

do that over home. We got the ways, but we ain't always got the means."

Garry laughed. "Neither have we, always. How's Shirley?"

"Better. She's cutting out paper dolls on the sofa. Mary wanted to know could you spare us a little coffee, 'cause I won't be gettin' down to the store till around supper time. And I thought I'd just take a look how your woodpile was holdin' out. I guess there's likely to be a cold snap coming on most any day, now."

"More snow?" Kay asked.

"It's banking up for that, by the looks of it. The way I figure it, we'll get a good old-fashioned snowfall, an' then our cold weather'll follow right back of it. If we do, Garry, I'll get the old sleigh out and we'll all go sleigh riding. Pack all the kids in and have a real family party."

"Grand!"

Kay didn't look so happy. "Do you mean it'll get colder than this?"

"Why, we haven't had any real cold yet," Neal told her. "Not what I call cold. This here is just mild ordinary winter weather. You wait and see."

That evening Garry, looking through a pile of papers and magazines that she was tidying up, stopped to re-read a few lines that had caught her eye.

[99]

"Listen, Kay. Look at this. Here's the very thing we want."

It was a copy of a weekly literary review that had come with some other magazines from Cousin Caroline, who remembered the country relatives from time to time when papers accumulated. Garry pointed to the advertisement at the foot of one column:

> WANTED. By writer, quiet room and plain board with country family, or would share small cottage. Working privacy essential. Reasonable. Z.Y.3.

"You mean a sort of paying guest? You're crazy!"

"I'm not. It would settle our whole question. Listen. She can have the parlor here. It's warm and quiet, we'll fix it up nicely and she can shut herself in and write all day if she wants to. And she can have meals with us, or separately. If she wants privacy she needn't see anything of us if she doesn't want to; so much the better. That means we won't have to do any entertaining or bothering about her. And it would be someone staying in the house, too, and that will stop Penny worrying—you know she did, last letter, about our being alone here. And instead of us paying her, she'll be paying us. I think it's a swell idea!"

Garry threw the paper down with her characteristic

air of having decided everything, once and for all.

"But Garry—we don't know a thing about the kind of person she is, even. Suppose it's someone terribly fussy?"

"Only nice people would advertise in that kind of paper, anyway," said Garry firmly. "And if she's fussy, she can't be any fussier than the Cummings was. It says plain board, and heaven knows our board is plain enough to please anyone. When she's here, maybe we can afford to have it a little fancier. What date is that paper?"

Kay turned it over.

"Three weeks old."

"Never mind. There's always a chance she hasn't found anything to suit her yet. Kay, we'll have to get that letter written tonight, right now."

Garry began to rummage in the desk for paper and envelopes.

"It mightn't be such a bad idea," Kay considered. "If we only knew . . ."

"Knew what?" Garry's head lifted impatiently. "I tell you it's a swell idea. Sit down here. How would you begin?"

Kay thought it over, staring at the sheet of paper in front of her.

"Dear Madam, having seen your advertisement . . ."

"No," said Garry after a moment. "That's what everybody would write. We don't want to sound like a tea room or a boarding house. Leave this to me, Kay. We've got to write something that will make her interested, to start with."

She took a pad and pencil and settled herself in the sofa corner, overalled knees drawn up to her chin as usual in moments of deep thought.

"Don't put a whole lot of stuff that will make her think the place nicer than it is," Kay advised, beginning after the first shock to get really interested.

"What do you think I am? I'm going to tell her the worst, then there won't be any come-backs."

For ten minutes Garry scribbled, with many pauses and a good deal of scratching out. Presently she said: "Listen to this:

"Dear Z.Y.3,

"If you really want a place in the country where you can write in peace and quiet we have a comfortable ground-floor room, with open fireplace. We are four in the family, and my sister is an artist. This is genuine country. We have no modern conveniences except the telephone. You could have plain meals either with us or by yourself and we can undertake that you will not be disturbed in your work unless you want to be, because we are usually pretty busy ourselves. There is no radio and we are seven miles from the railroad. We like it here and I think that you would.

> "Yours sincerely,
> "Margaret Ellis.

"And a darn good letter too, I call it."

"Why did you say that about me?" Kay objected.

"To show her the sort of people we are. She'd want to know, if she's going to live with us. And you can't say I haven't been strictly truthful."

"You've been too truthful," Kay groaned. "Do you suppose anyone in their senses would want to come here, after reading that?"

"Anyone like you or me would. Like me, anyway. And most writers hate radios; that's why I said we hadn't got one. So she won't have that to worry about."

"She'll have plenty else! You never said what we would charge."

"Do I have to? I thought she'd say that. Good Lord, Kay, what should we charge?"

"Five dollars a week?"

"You're nuts. Fifteen is more like it."

"Garry, we *can't!* There isn't even a bathroom."

"I sort of hinted as much, didn't I? There's our old zinc tub in the kitchen, and we'll include Cousin Carrie's bath salts, free. Now listen here. This has got to cover our grocery bill, don't forget. Down at that farm over near the lake they charge sixteen a week; Mary told me. But they give you cream, and we don't have cream. Suppose we charge her fourteen? That's fifty-six dollars a month, and if you're a writer and want peace and quiet—and that's what she's willing to pay for—you just try living anywhere for fifty-six dollars a month, and see what you get!"

"It seems an awful lot to me."

"We've got to be businesslike," said Garry. And she added at the foot of the letter: "Would fourteen dollars a week be too much?"

It was not until after the letter, duly copied and addressed in Garry's square sturdy hand, had been stamped and left on the mantelpiece for next morning's mail, and Garry herself was just dropping off to sleep in bed, the covers pulled up to her ears, that there came a dubious whisper from across the dark room.

"Garry . . . I was thinking. That advertisement never said it was a woman. Suppose it's a man?"

Garry's voice was muffled by blankets.

"All the better. If it's a man we can make him chop our kindling for us. He'll want some sort of exercise."

Kay sighed.

"Well, I suppose we'll know when we get an answer. If we ever do."

But a good deal was to happen before that answer came.

VI

Winterbound

NEAL was right. Next morning there was an ominous grayness in the air. By midday the snow began to fall, first in big whirling flakes, then closer and denser, shutting out the landscape like a white curtain, packing against the door sill and drifting high in the hollows. The children came home from school shouting and red-cheeked, snow clinging thickly to their clothing and sifted down their necks, shaking themselves like dogs as they ran in through the door that Garry held ajar against the rising wind.

"There's four inches now. If it keeps up Jimmy says we won't get down to the state road tomorrow, not unless they get the snow plows out."

It did keep up. Garry and Martin worked hard bringing in armloads of wood before the big outdoor woodpile should get snowed under, till their fingers were frozen through their wet gloves.

"Gosh, there's enough here to last us through a blizzard!" Martin exclaimed, dropping his last heavy load on the shed floor.

"So you think," said Garry darkly. It was her job to tend Big Bertha and she knew how much that monster ate.

By supper time the snow had piled halfway up the windowpanes on the north side of the house, and when Caroline pulled the curtain aside it was to peer out on a white and buried world.

There was no going to school next day. The kitchen door opened onto a snowbank, and Martin stepped out above his knees. Jimmie brought the milk over a good hour later than usual, floundering through unbroken drifts, and between them they shoveled a narrow path as far as the mailbox. Later Neal hitched his two horses to the homemade snow plow, three heavy timbers spiked together to make a rough triangle, and the boys and Caroline clung squealing to the back bar while it swung and slithered down the hill, breaking a track and pushing the snow into high banks against either side of the road.

Down on the lower road the town plow was busily forging its way, an impressive yellow monster that threw the loose snow up in showers as it chugged along. Neal, about to turn his horses at the foot of the hill, drew up and waited with the children to see it pass.

"Hey, what you tryin' to do—spoil the sledding?" he shouted as the engine drew abreast.

The driver grinned back.

"Better take them horses off of the road before we scrape 'em up!"

Road and hedgerow shimmered through the hot air from the exhaust. The horses' breath came in white clouds as they stood waiting. Neal's sturdy figure planted with feet braced well apart on the snow plow, the children in their knitted caps and mufflers, old Sam, the Walker hound, sitting down beside them with his tongue lolling out—the whole made a cheerful picture, sharp cut against the heaped sparkling snow.

"Me an' my horses, we're making a decent job of it," Neal drawled. "By the time you're finished muckin' up the road bed with that yaller pushcart we'll have to get to work an' pay for havin' it all put back again."

"Oh yeah? Didn't see you at the Grange dance Friday night."

"You didn't. My best an' me was all fixed up to go, but she turned it down at the last minute. Seems she heard you was goin' to be there. Bad news always gets around, some way. Giddap, Dolly!"

The horses swung round into the cleared road, making a wide circle. The snow-plow driver leaned out and waved. Then they were breasting the hill again, the heavy wooden frame lurching like a ship at sea while the children clung to one another to keep their balance.

"Good as toboggan ridin'," said Neal. "Hang on tight. When we get back I'll take a turn round the barn and then we're through. I'll clear you a nice track there for sleddin' on."

The horses pawed and floundered through the drifts on the pasture slope, where the plow left a wide curving track, smooth and close packed for the sleds to run on, with a soft snow bank on either side.

The bright clear cold was growing steadily colder by afternoon, and a steely haze crept over the hills. Neither of the boys wanted to give up coasting, but Caroline left them early and came back to warm her pink chilled hands at the stove.

Kay was deep in her rug, sorting colors by the window.

"Had enough sledding, Caroline?"

"I guess so."

"Then take your things off quickly. The snow's just dripping off you!"

Caroline began to tug in a half-hearted way. She was so long about it that Garry had to come and help.

"Anything happened out there?"

"No. . . . I just got tired."

"You're all chilled through," said Garry briskly.

"You should have had sense enough to come in before."
Caroline flounced aside.

"I'm not. I'm burning hot, if you want to know. And I guess my head aches, too."

Kay and Garry exchanged glances.

"I'll tuck you up on the sofa and you can take a nap till supper time."

In spite of Big Bertha the windowpanes were already beginning to freeze over, earlier than they had ever done before. Garry scratched a fingernail across the transparent ice. "Look at that already! It's going to be pretty cold tonight."

"Five degrees now," cried Martin excitedly when he came in, cheeks burned red with the frost. "And it's going down all the time. Neal says it'll drop way below zero tonight."

Caroline felt no better by supper time. She was cross and irritable, drank a glass of hot milk under protest and was tucked up in her bed, which had long ago been shifted into the room where her sisters slept, warmed by the floor register just above Bertha's towering head. That register made an isle of comfort on which to dress or undress in chilly weather, and the girls were doubly glad of it tonight.

"I'll make up a good big fire that'll keep till morning," Garry said.

WINTERBOUND

She wedged chunk after chunk into Bertha's cavernous mouth before closing the drafts. But the wind changed during the night; instead of smoldering as they should the logs burned themselves out and when Garry came down in the early morning there was only a handful of graying ashes left. A chill light filtered through the ice-covered windows. In the kitchen everything was frozen solid.

Garry gave one grim look around her, pulled on a windbreaker, and went out in the shed to split fresh kindling, for Martin had forgotten his job in the excitement of sledding yesterday and the wood-box was nearly empty. The pump handle only gave a dismal croak when she took hold of it, but luckily there was still water—or rather ice—in the kettle. She got the kitchen fire started, set the frozen coffeepot over it, and returned to struggle with Bertha.

Martin heard her stirring and stumbled drowsily out in bathrobe and slippers, his teeth chattering.

"What's happening? Did the fire go out?"

"Oh, no! I'm just trying to keep the heat down!"

Ashes were flying in the room. Garry, poker in hand, turned a smudgy and exasperated face on him.

"Wrap a blanket around you and go sit by the kitchen stove till I come—and keep it *going*. And watch that coffeepot. I'll be right out."

WINTERBOUND

She laid fresh kindling over the still warm ashes, with a fresh log on top, and opened the drafts. Bertha could be depended upon to do her best.

Martin was peering into the percolator. "Do you suppose frozen coffee's bad for one?"

"No, of course it isn't; I've drunk it dozens of times," Garry knew her Martin; he had a horrible memory for scraps of information read in newspapers, especially relating to what he called "chemical reactions." The slightest hesitation on her part, and that precious coffee would have gone straight into the slop pail. She snatched the pot from him barely in time and set it back on the stove. "There's enough for us two there and I'll make some fresh as soon as the water's thawed out. You get some cups out and for heaven's sake don't make any racket; I want Kay to go on sleeping till the house has warmed up."

The kitchen stove was burning cheerfully by now; they sat with their feet on the oven ledge and drank the left-over coffee while little by little the room grew warmer and tiny misted spots appeared on the window-panes.

"Thirty-six," said Garry presently, going to look at the thermometer which hung by the doorway between the two rooms. "Lord knows what it's like outside."

They were to look at that thermometer many times

before the day was out. Neal's cold snap had come with a vengeance. Martin was all set to go to school in spite of the temperature, but learning when Neal came over with the milk that Jimmy was staying home, he thought better of it, and spent the morning across the way instead. Even that short dash across the road made him feel like an arctic explorer.

"Eighteen below last night," Neal told them. "Mary and I sat up all night to keep the fires going. It's all of ten below now, or I miss my guess. No sense letting those kids walk down to the school bus and back this weather."

And yet there was something exhilarating in the cold, Garry thought when she went out into the yard and felt the keen sting of the air against her face, a sort of excitement in knowing what real winter weather could be like.

Kay was worried about Caroline, who huddled near the stove, listless and shivering. Her cheeks were burning and her hands cold and clammy.

"It's a straight old-fashioned cold," said Garry. "If Penny were here she'd give her a good dose of something and put her back to bed. I'll light the drum stove upstairs and we'll get the room good and warm before she goes up."

For once Caroline made no objection to anything. All she wanted was to curl up in bed and lie there, and it was this unwonted submissiveness more than anything else that frightened her sisters.

"If only I knew what she felt like, I'd know more what to do," Kay said helplessly. But Caroline wouldn't even tell them what she felt like. She lay and snuffled into her handkerchief, refusing all comfort and only wanting Penny—Penny who had always been on hand every time before when she felt sick.

And Penny was in New Mexico.

Garry went over to the Rowes, sure strength in all emergencies, and returned with Mary and the clinical thermometer.

"Hundred and a half," said Mary. "I don't believe it's anything more than a cold. You could call the doctor up, but he'd have eight miles to drive and the roads are awful. Neal says there'll be hardly a car out today. I tell you what. If her temperature goes up, or if she isn't any better by tomorrow, why don't you call Miss Hussey? She's the district nurse."

"Would she come?"

"Of course she'll come. And she hasn't so far to drive, either. I'd as soon have her as anyone. She was grand when Shirley was sick last spring. And if you need a doctor she'll tell you right away. I'll write her number down for you, and I'll leave the thermometer here."

She went, and the little wave of reassurance she had brought somehow vanished with her.

"Do you suppose it *is* anything?" Kay worried.

"Anything" meant pneumonia, Garry knew. That unspoken word hung in the air between them.

"She'd have a worse temperature than that, if it was."

Miss Hussey, over the telephone, sounded cheerful and unperturbed. There were a lot of bad colds going about just now. Keep the little girl in bed, and she would come over and have a look at her tomorrow.

"Well, I suppose that's all we can do," said Kay.

She went upstairs to sit with Caroline. She found *Alice in Wonderland* on the bookshelves and began to read to her, but in the middle of the Hatter's tea party the print began to dance up and down before her eyes; her teeth chattered and she was conscious of a steadily growing ache through all her limbs. When Garry came up with a cup of hot tea it was to find two patients instead of one.

"I g-guess it's flu all right," Kay said. "I've had it before. Anyway we know what it is, now."

"Everything *would* happen at once," Garry thought, as she tucked Kay, too, into bed and marched down to fetch the thermometer and fill fresh hot-water bottles. The kitchen fire had gone down by the time she had Kay fairly settled; the pump was frozen up again and when she did get water boiling at last the kettle tipped over the

[116]

open stove hole and scalded her wrist as she made a hasty grab to catch it.

Martin ran for the olive oil in the pantry, but that too was a solid lump in the bottle, so all she could do was to smear butter on, biting her lip as Martin wound a bandage round with shaking fingers.

"That'll be all right; I don't give a hoot if it *is* septic—it takes the pain out anyway. Now pull my sleeve down—ouch! Thank goodness it's my left hand, or we'd be in a worse fix yet."

It was colder than ever that night. With Kay and Caroline in bed there seemed a gloom over the house. Garry and Martin ate their supper by the stove, and as she glanced at the windows Garry remembered those early winter days when they had asked one another: "Do you suppose it ever gets much colder than this?" This cold was like a living enemy. It seemed to prowl round the house, pushing at the door sills, snatching at every possible cranny to get in, and if it weren't for the snow which had sealed many of the cracks it would have been worse yet.

No taking chances on the stoves tonight, Garry decided. With Martin's help she dragged the sofa across the floor, cautiously so as not to wake Kay and Caroline upstairs; Martin brought a mattress and blankets from his own room and together they camped in the circle of Big

Bertha's comforting glow, like sentries round a camp fire.

"Aren't you going to undress?" Martin asked.

"Not tonight." She lit the stable lantern, set it on the floor by the stairway with the wick turned low, and lay down on the sofa with her clothes on and the old red comforter from the spare room wrapped about her.

"Then I won't sleep either."

"Don't be silly," said Garry.

The shadows stretched high on the walls, making queer pictures among the cracks and bulges of the old plaster. Now and again a log shifted in Big Bertha's interior, sending a little tongue of flame leaping up the stovepipe. Out in the pantry a rat, undismayed by the cold, was gnawing busily. Garry's wrist began to bother her. At the time she had been too busy to notice it much, but now the warmth was bringing out the pain.

Martin, for all his determination to keep her company, soon fell asleep, the blankets hugged tightly around him, but Garry lay long awake, watchful for a movement in the room above her, listening, as night drew on and the cold grew more intense, to the strange snapping and creaking of the frost outside—sudden sharp cracks and muffled thuds, as though the house itself were fighting desperately in the grip of the enemy, its old timbers about to fly apart at any moment. Frightening sounds to one who had never heard them before. They seemed to come from underfoot, from all around. One, louder than the rest, cracked like a pistol shot on the stillness, and in the dim light from the lantern she saw Martin's face, startled and wide-eyed, raised from his mattress.

"What was that?"

"Only the frost cracking, I guess. Go to sleep again." He snuggled under the blankets.

"I don't like it. Say . . . Garry?"

"What?"

"Suppose the whole house was to crack up?"

"It won't. I guess it's stood worse frosts than this."

She got up to put more wood on the kitchen stove and crept halfway up the stairs to listen if Kay or Caroline was stirring. But there was no sound; only the queer watchful emptiness of the house about her, the crackling of the frost outside. It was just two o'clock. She pulled the covers round her once more and settled back to doze.

When she opened her eyes again it was daylight. Martin was awake before her: he had set the kettle over and made fresh coffee. In his anxiety to have it good and strong he had used double measure and let the percolator bubble frantically; Garry winced at the first bitter mouthful, but it did her good.

WINTERBOUND

Kay's fever had gone down, but she felt weak and miserable. Martin was a tower of strength that morning, helpful as only a boy can be when he suddenly realizes a crisis in the familiar machinery of home life. He brought in wood, swept up the living room, washed the dishes, and kept looking anxiously at Garry as though he expected her, too, at any moment to keel over before his eyes. As a matter of fact she wasn't feeling any too good herself; her head was buzzing, the floor had a tendency to rise and drop unexpectedly under her feet as she moved about, and more than once she paused in what she was doing to clench her teeth and mutter angrily: "Garry Ellis, just pull yourself together, you blame fool. You *can't* get sick now."

The morning dragged by and at midday, when Garry had almost given up hope of her, Miss Hussey arrived. The mere sight of her brought comfort. She was stout and motherly and deliberate in her movements. She took off her numerous outer wrappings, unpacked her little black bag on the table, tied a fresh apron over her uniform, and went out into the kitchen to peer into the kettle and poke the fire up, chatting to Garry about the weather and asking after the Rowes (particularly Shirley and Tommy, both of whom, it seemed, she had helped to bring into the world)—as though driving six miles over ice-bound roads in zero weather to look after a family of strangers were quite an everyday matter, as it doubtless was to her.

"Good thing Neal Rowe got that road plowed out before it froze up on him," she remarked cheerfully, "or I'd have had a hard job getting up here, chains or no chains. It wouldn't be the first time they've had to pull me out of the drifts, either. Sure as we get a real hard cold spell or a big snowfall, someone up the back roads gets sick. I never knew it to fail. And this road's nothing to where I have to go, sometimes."

Upstairs she took temperatures, straightened beds, and shook pillows with a masterly hand. She gave Caroline a hospital bath from head to foot, which filled that young person with a sense of great importance and did much to raise her spirits, and she rubbed Kay's aching limbs with alcohol.

"Now I guess you're all set for a while," she said when she rejoined Garry downstairs. "I'll look in again day after tomorrow if you need me, but I guess you won't. Keep that child indoors till after the cold spell's over, and don't let your sister there get up till she has to. Two or three days in bed ought to put her straight again. How do you feel yourself?"

"All right," said Garry.

WINTERBOUND

The shrewd eyes rested on her approvingly.

"Don't overdo it, and if you get any temperature go right to bed and call me up. We don't want you sick, too, if we can help it. What did you do to your wrist, burn it?"

"The kettle spilled over."

"I'll fix it for you." She unbuckled her bag once more to take out salve and a roll of bandage. "There's nothing like cold weather for things happening. A day like this it seems like all your fingers are thumbs and everything you take hold of either spills on you or cuts you or you drop it on your toe. That feel any better?"

"It certainly does. Thanks a lot." Garry pulled her sleeve down gratefully over the cool soft dressing. "I . . . we . . . Mary didn't say what we owed you for coming."

"Fifty cents," said Miss Hussey briskly, buttoning up her coat.

She picked up her little bag again and was gone, driving off down the hill to visit other households in affliction, leaving comfort and cheer behind her.

For five more days the frost held. Kay and Caroline were up and about again but there was no going out except for Martin, who spent long hours skating with Jimmie on the little pond at the foot of the hill. Life was a monotonous round of watching the thermometer and tending stoves.

WINTERBOUND

On the sixth night Garry woke up towards dawn with a sudden queer sensation of something having happened, an unfamiliar feeling in the air. Sitting up in the darkness, it took her a full minute to realize what it was. The cold spell had finally broken.

VII

Garry Finds a Job

FREEZING still, but the bitterness had gone from the air. It was good to stand outdoors again, to be able to draw breath freely.

Edna drove over to see them. She had telephoned twice during the combined cold-and-flu siege to ask how they were getting along, but had not been able to visit.

"Just a lame shoulder," she explained, "but I wouldn't have dared try and hold the wheel straight over these roads. But I was bound to get up and see you all today, even if I had to drive with my teeth!"

Edna was resplendent in a new hat, a new scarf and sweater, and a pair of smart fur-lined driving gloves, a Christmas gift from one of her devoted "old ladies."

"I put everything on to show you," she laughed. "I got a pair of red bedroom slippers, too, and if it wasn't for driving I'd have worn them. And that reminds me: back in the car there's a Christmas present we got and

couldn't keep, because we've two like it already, so I
brought it along for Caroline."

"Couldn't you get it exchanged?" Kay asked.

"Not this one you can't. It comes in all sizes, but only
one make." She went back to the car and returned carrying a square grocer's carton tied securely with twine.
"Open it and see."

Garry cut the string. There was a stirring and rustling
inside, and a black suspicious nose poked out from a nest
of tissue paper.

"A coon kitten from the state of Maine," said Edna.
"My aunt and uncle up there have more cats than you
can shake a stick at. Every so often they send us one down.
He runs a dairy farm there, and the barns are simply running with cats. Summer visitors always like them, so they
get rid of a few that way. Uncle is always talking about
getting his gun and clearing some of those cats out, but
when it comes right down to it he wouldn't touch a hair
of 'em, and there's plenty of milk and scraps going, so
I guess they don't bother anyone much. This 'un looked
real smart to me, but we've two cats already and that's
too many for anyone living in town. I wish clothes lasted
as long as cats do! Our old Susie will be thirteen next
month."

The coon kitten had hoisted himself out of the carton
and was beginning a wary tour of the room. His long

thick hair was jet black all over, his eyes a deep glowing amber. While Garry ran for a saucer of milk Kay exclaimed:

"Caroline will love him. He's just like a Persian, only prettier. Are they always that color?"

"Black or yellow, mostly. Though there was a grand black and white with white paws I remember as a child; he used to run wild in the woods back of the house and no one could ever get near him. You'd just get a glimpse of him sometimes, along towards fall when the hunting began to grow scarce. Aunt has a family of yellow ones, too, but the yellow kittens mostly get picked up by the summer folk. Either black or yellow's a good color for cats in the country; if you have one of these grays or tabbies they're like to get taken for a rabbit or a squirrel some fine day, and you lose 'em. Neal Rowe's more careful with his gun than most, but there's lots of hunters don't bother to look twice when they see something moving."

Caroline had gone back to school that day for the first time. Edna had brought sliced ham and a home-baked pie, so the three of them ate lunch together in the living room while the coon kitten prowled and explored.

"I thought I'd kill two birds with one stone today," Edna said as she drank her third cup of coffee. "There was a job up this way I'd heard about, but I guess I can't take it. It's the woman down here on the state road, right opposite the milk station where the school bus stops. They've got a little nursery business called Roadside— raise flowers and seedlings. We always get our tomato and pepper plants from them in spring. The husband's lame. She had her first baby a few days ago—right in the middle of that cold spell it was—and her sister was staying there but now she's had to go home and they wanted someone to look after things round the house till Mrs. Collins gets about again. But it would mean going there every day, and I can't manage it."

"I didn't know you took jobs," Kay said.

"Anything I can get, when the taxi business is slack. I clean folks' summer cottages and close up for them, and I do spring cleaning once in a while. When you live in the country you learn to turn your hand to most anything. I felt sorry about these folks—she's a real nice woman— but the most I can do is to try and find someone else for them."

There was the latest Santa Fé news to be told, scraps from Penny's letters to be read aloud; all the exchange of local and family gossip that always took place on Edna's visits. When at last she rose to go Garry said:

"Guess I'll ride down the road with you a little way, and walk back."

She pulled on rubber boots and a windbreaker. When they were halfway down the hill she said:

GARRY'S JOB

"I'm going after that job myself, if I can get it."

Edna smiled as her foot pressed down on the brake.

"Good for you. I can drop you right there. She'll be pretty glad."

"What does it mean?"

"Housework, getting the dinner—maybe a little washing. Miss Hussey comes in every day, so you won't have much to do with the baby."

"I guess I can do all that. I don't know an awful lot about cooking, but she can tell me how she wants things done."

"I always said you'd fit in anywhere, all right," Edna said. "You see, there isn't much of regular hired help around here, but when folks are in a fix anyone will do what they can. I guess they haven't got an awful lot of money, but she's willing to pay ten dollars a week."

"That's ten dollars more than I ever earned before," Garry returned. "Just the other day I was saying that there wasn't any way to earn money in the country, and here it is. Only I didn't want to say anything in front of Kay—not till I know whether I've got the job or not."

There was another reason too perhaps, which Edna perfectly understood.

"I remember as well as yesterday," she said as they turned the corner into the lower road, "the time I was fourteen and I wanted to get a new dress for the church picnic where we lived, and I didn't have more'n a few cents saved up for it. So I marched off and hired me out, to a woman that took in boarders, to wash dishes and clean the kitchen up twice a day. My aunt was staying on a visit with us, and the way she carried on when she heard about it you'd have thought there was something disgraceful in washing other folks' dishes instead of one's own. But my mother was the sensible kind. She said: 'If Edna wants money let her set to and earn it, and then it'll mean something to her. As long as there's dishes to wash I never heard that it mattered what house you wash 'em in, so long as you wash 'em clean.' So I got my dress, and a nice dress it was, too. I spent all of eight dollars on it, and that was a lot in those days."

When Garry reached home a couple of hours later, having trudged the long steep hill road with more buoyancy and self-confidence than she had felt in some time, she found Martin and Caroline already back from school. She entered whistling, tossed her cap on the table and announced:

"Well, I've got a job!"

Caroline was too absorbed in the coon kitten to pay any attention, but Martin lifted his head.

"What job?" And Kay exclaimed: "Garry, not that job Edna was talking about? I might have known you were up to something when you sneaked off that way. You can't do that sort of thing!"

Garry's chin went up.

"I don't see why. It wouldn't be the first time an Ellis turned her lily-white hands to something useful. And I want to tell you that I feel right like a million dollars this minute. I never knew anything could give one such a lift. The only thing is I hate to take their money for doing just everyday things, because I don't believe by the look of the place they've got a cent more than they can manage with, and the woman is a dear. She's young and pretty—she looks a little bit like you, Kay—and the baby's a darling; I never saw anything so tiny! If you'd been there yourself, Kay, you wouldn't have thought twice about it. She was sitting up in bed there with a pink jacket on, with the baby tucked up in a clothes basket beside her, and she was peeling potatoes and hushing the baby at the same time. When I said what I'd come for she acted kind of scared of me at first because she'd heard we were city people, till I told her all about the family and how we were fixed, and I took the potatoes right out of her hands and started doing them myself, for I thought I'd show her I could do that much, anyway."

Garry smiled, remembering the expression on Mrs. Collins's face when the potato bowl was whisked away so promptly. Edna had sensibly refused to come in, feeling that Garry would make her way better alone, as she certainly had. But it was the baby who had really settled the question, for Garry adored all small things, and the sight of her eager face bent over the clothes basket had outweighed any last doubts Mrs. Collins might have had about "city people."

"Ten dollars a week, and I start tomorrow. I wish it would last all winter, but it won't. Still, it's given me a good idea. If I suit all right I shall get Mrs. Collins to give me a reference. In the country people are always having babies and if I keep in touch with Miss Hussey I might get a lot more jobs when this one's over."

Kay had to laugh, for Garry's ideas always spread in widening circles like a stone thrown into water.

"Wait till you see how you like this one. Are you really sure you want it?"

But Garry was quite serious, even though it meant getting up early every morning to walk the mile and a half to the state road. There was a thrill in having a job of any kind for the first time, and she was still young enough to feel work in another person's house more of an adventure than a task. She washed dishes, scrubbed pantry shelves, swept floors and cooked dinner in a businesslike way; she did the baby's laundry without wincing; and she even learned to sterilize feeding bottles and to prepare formulas as though she had been used to it all her life. Miss

Hussey, coming in on her visit to bathe the baby, gave
her a friendly approving smile.

"Well, well, so you've got a new job these days! Not
enough to do up home, huh? How's the family?"

"All fine. Caroline's back at school again."

"Good."

Garry enjoyed these daily visits. She liked Miss Hussey's brisk cheery ways and amusing gossip, and hurried
to get her work forward so that she could watch the
bathing and dressing rites. It was all good experience, for
she had never had anything to do with a baby as tiny as
this, and she learned a lot that she had not known before.
Anything small and young Garry loved; baby animals,
baby plants, she was used to tending and handling, but
this human specimen was something new and every detail
of its care absorbed her.

Mrs. Collins, her first shyness worn off, was friendly
and talkative, glad of Garry's company as well as her
help. Both she and her husband were newcomers in the
neighborhood; before their marriage Mr. Collins had
worked for a firm of nursery gardeners and had only
started in business for himself three years ago. He was a
kindly, rather silent man, lame from a shell wound in
the War; Garry rarely saw him except at mealtimes, or
when he tiptoed in once or twice during the morning to
look at the baby and perhaps stroke its small hand gently

with the tip of one finger as though it were some rare and delicate seedling that he was almost afraid to touch. Most of the time he was busy in the greenhouse or potting shed.

Garry longed to talk to him about his work but never quite found the courage. The greenhouse where he raised his plants and cuttings had been built onto the house and opened directly from the small living room; as Garry stood at the kitchen sink rinsing clothes or washing dishes she could see the rows of flowerpots behind the glass panes and whenever the door was opened a warm breath of earth and moisture filled the house. Many a time she was sorely tempted to cross the floor and open that door herself, just to take a sniff and look inside, but she reminded herself sternly that she was there to do chores and keep house, not to indulge her own particular hobby. Still the temptation was very strong and one morning she gave in to it. Her hands happened to be still soapy; the doorhandle slipped unexpectedly in her grasp and she all but fell down the two steps on to Mr. Collins's broad back as he stooped over a tray on the lower shelf. He looked taken aback at this entry but relieved to find it was not an urgent summons for help, and grinned as he pulled her to her feet.

"Those steps are a bit tricky when you aren't used to 'em," he said. "Did you hurt yourself any?"

GARRY'S JOB

"Not a bit. I'm awfully sorry, but I just had a minute to spare and I've so wanted to have a look at your plants. I love greenhouses and I hardly ever get a chance to poke round in them."

"Look at all you want to," said Mr. Collins.

He stopped his work goodnaturedly to show her round, explained how the house was heated and the moisture controlled, let her linger over the rows of potted seedlings and the cuttings set to root in trays of wet sand. Following him as he limped down the aisle between the growing plants Garry found that here was a man who loved his work and could forget all his awkwardness in talking about it. She was full of eager questions and real understanding, and the time flew till she suddenly remembered the potatoes on the stove and the unset dinner table.

After that she was free of the greenhouse whenever there were odd moments to spare, and as Mrs. Collins was now sitting up and the district nurse's visits becoming fewer, Garry could generally manage by working at extra speed to gain a little time. When the baby was fed and sleeping, Mrs. Collins settled for her afternoon nap, and the dishes put away, she would slip out and help Mr. Collins. There were plants to spray and water, sometimes seedlings to be re-potted or rooted cuttings set out, empty pots to be scrubbed and stacked away, or potting mold

[135]

mixed in the big trough at the end of the greenhouse—
jobs she enjoyed far more than scraping saucepans and
mopping floors.

"Well, I'll give you a regular job any time you want
it," he said one day jokingly, and Garry took him up at
once.

"Would you let me work here, if you want extra help
later on?"

"Well, there's always plenty to do, come spring. But I
don't know as you'd call it a young lady's work, exactly,
except once in a while like now, when you feel in the
mood." He seemed to overlook entirely the kind of work
Garry had been doing, this last week. "Handlin' earth
and pots an' that isn't any too good on your hands."

"I've handled plenty," Garry told him. "I'm only a
beginner, Mr. Collins, and I wouldn't want you to pay
me. But there's a whole lot I could learn working with
you, and I'd be glad to do it. I could take care of some
of the easier jobs and leave you more time for the rest."

Mr. Collins considered.

"There's rock-garden plants," he said. "Folks are
crazy about them, right now. If I had money it would
pay me to go in for the real Alpines, but there's plenty
others that I'm beginning to have a steady sale for, for
there's one thing they can't always raise from a packet of
seed. Divisions they increase from, mostly. I've got a lot

of young plants on hand in the cold-frames and I thought I might do a good bit in that line this year. That'll call for a lot of dividing and settin' out, and I don't know but you might try your hand at that, if you'd care to. But we'll see later on. Come spring you'll have plenty doing in your own garden."

"I couldn't get a promise out of him," she told Kay that evening, "but I mean to try again in the spring. It's just the chance I need and I don't mean to let it slip."

There was little doing in the way of business at Roadside Nurseries just now. So far not a single customer had stopped by during the week that Garry had spent there, but towards the end of her stay one car actually did draw up, a smart sedan with two well-dressed women in it. Mr. Collins had gone to town that afternoon; Mrs. Collins was giving the baby her two-o'clock bottle, and Garry had just finished her third batch of diapers and was hanging them on the line behind the kitchen stove.

"Good afternoon. I got such nice cyclamens here last year, and my friend was wondering if you had any more."

Mrs. Collins looked flustered.

"Mr. Collins would know, but he's out just now. That's too bad. I suppose you couldn't . . ."

Garry turned promptly.

"There are some nice ones just coming into bloom. Would you like to see them?"

WINTERBOUND

She left the washtub, gave a businesslike hitch to her
overalls, and led the way into the greenhouse. Roadside
Nurseries wasn't going to miss its one sale of the week if
she could help it.

"They're down at the end here. Mr. Collins had to go
into town to see about a new consignment of plants, but
I expect I can help you just as well."

Mr. Collins's trip had been to arrange for a renewal of
his bank loan, as Garry very well knew, being by now
practically a member of the family, but that explanation
wouldn't sound quite so impressive. The cyclamens
(Garry thanked heaven it was an everyday plant she
did know, not something unusual with a long Latin
name) were on a warm shelf at the far end of the house,
and she led her visitors purposely by the aisle where the
best-looking plants and seedlings were ranged. The elder
of the two women happened to be a genuine gardener;
she had taken a fancy to Garry's voice and appearance and
was inclined to linger more than once on the way to chat
about this or that.

"They're all very nice," said the younger woman presently, as Garry reached down pot after pot to set before
her. "I don't like dark red so much, do you, Mary?
There's a white one up there . . . is that the only one
you have? It looks rather . . ."

Garry patiently took the last pot down from its shelf.

"The only one; I'm sorry. But this pale pink is lovely, and it's full of buds. It ought to be perfect in just a few days." (What, oh what did Mr. Collins charge for cyclamens?)

The young woman still hemmed and hawed, turning the pots about.

"I saw some just like this in town. They were asking forty-five cents. Isn't that what you paid last year, Mary?"

Garry looked at the elder woman's smooth ringed hands, at her companion's costly fur coat, and thought of the Collins baby, asleep at this moment in a clothes basket under two cheap cotton blankets.

"These are seventy-five cents each," she said firmly. "They ought to be more, really, but they're the last we have."

"That seems very dear, doesn't it?"

"Detestable female!" thought Garry, and added aloud: "These are particularly well-grown plants, Mr. Collins won't stock anything that isn't good."

"Hm. . . ." Her eyes rested on Garry inquisitively. "Do you work here all the time?"

"Only when Mr. Collins is short-handed."

In the end she chose three after much deliberation, while the elder woman, left to wander by herself, had discovered other things that she wanted. Garry swathed the pots carefully, carried them out to the back of the car, and returned proudly to lay six dollars and a fifty-cent piece on the baby's blanket.

"That'll help to buy her something useful, I guess!"

"How much did you dare charge them?"

"Seventy-five for the cyclamens and two dollars each for the little evergreens. There are plenty more of the same kind, but those two happened to be standing all by themselves and she took a shine to them. She was so pleased I was scared after that I'd undercharged her, but I'm pretty sure I didn't," said Garry. "And I let her have a strawberry begonia for a quarter, just to make up."

"The first sale in ages." Mrs. Collins smiled gratefully. "Wait till George hears about it. I guess you brought us luck!"

"The older woman will be back again; she said so, and she likes the place. She's interested in rock plants, too. I wouldn't care if we never saw the other one again. Wearing a three-hundred-dollar coat and wants to save thirty cents on flowers!"

"Lots of 'em are that way," said Mrs. Collins, who had had experience. And she added: "I wish you could stay here always."

So did Garry. In these ten days she had come to feel so much a part of the little household that when she pulled her rubber boots on for the last time, hung up her apron, and stooped to kiss the small curled fist lying outside the covers it seemed as if she was leaving a part of herself behind. It was with an empty almost homesick feeling that she climbed the hill that evening with ten dollars in her pocket (she had stubbornly refused to take more for the extra days), a promise to stand godmother to small Julia when the time came, and a store of new experience and self-confidence that was worth far more to her than any wages.

Much of the snow had melted, but a new light fall had come to cover the unsightly patches of bare earth. It was a soft misty night; there was no wind and though the mercury stood at just about freezing the air felt mild. Just the night for fox hunting, Neal announced. He had long promised the two boys a moonlight fox hunt, and the moon would rise about nine.

When Garry reached home she found Martin all excited. He fairly bolted his supper and was ready long before Neal and Jimmie knocked at the door.

"You wrap up well," Kay admonished.

"Walkin'll keep 'em warm," drawled Neal. "We ain't settin' out for the North Pole. That leather jacket's all you need, son, with a good sweater under it, and I bet you find that too much. I'll look out for him all right." He winked at the two girls. "Sorry you ain't coming, Garry. I reckon if we git one fox apiece that's all we'll want to carry, but maybe if we meet up with a fourth one and he's extra good, we might bring him back for you."

"I'll bet you don't get one!" Garry scoffed.

"Is that kind? Didn't I pick this night special? Moon just right, everything just right, and old Sam fairly bustin' hisself to get out on the job. Wait till you hear him singin', once he hits a good scent. We're goin' out over Crooked Hill and work round towards Bear Hollow and the big ledges. I ain't hunted over there yet this winter and I bet you we pick up something before we're through."

His deep leather pockets bulged with a package of sandwiches on one side and a thermos flask on the other. "See you later," he nodded as he picked up his gun from the corner by the door.

"Why didn't you go along?" Kay asked when the door had closed behind them.

"It's Martin's party," Garry said. "Besides, I don't like seeing things shot, even if Neal does the shooting. . . . Well, it seems funny to be home for keeps again." She opened the stove door and pushed a fresh log into Big Bertha. "Remember how we hated this stove when Penny first brought it home? I bet if there are any auctions in Santa Fé she's having the time of her life. Think

of all the things she'll want to bring back with her!—
Kay, I want to make something for that baby down the
road, and I've got to think what."

"There was that pink sweater wool," Kay debated.
"Only I gave it to Caroline to learn knitting with when
she was sick and I guess it's pretty mussy by now—what's
left of it."

"Uh-uh. I hate knitting anyway. I'll go and take a
look round."

She went upstairs, where Kay could hear her dragging
trunks out in the room overhead.

"Just the thing," she exclaimed when she came down
again. "That peach robe I got Christmas before last. The
front's worn but the back is all right, and I had it cleaned
just before we came up here. It'll make a grand cot
cover."

"Are you going to cut that up?" Kay looked ruefully
at the shimmering quilted silk.

"Can you see me trailing a peach silk negligee around
this place—or anywhere else for that matter! It's lamb's
wool inside, so it will be beautifully warm." She took the
scissors and began to slash. "If I piece a bit more in these
two top corners and just turn the edges in all round it
makes quite a good-size spread. I can use that pink sewing
silk out of your workbox. Kay, now that Penny has to
stay longer than she thought, don't you think it would be

fun to get the house fixed up a bit by the time she gets home?"

"I'd love to. Only . . ."

"There's this ten dollars; part of it anyway. I might get another job of some kind, and if we ever hear anything from our advertisement woman there'd be some of that money, too."

"She'd have written long ago if she was coming," Kay said. "We'll never hear from her."

"The old buzzard," Garry commented. "People just make me sick anyway. I think she might answer even if she isn't coming." She spread the silk out, viewing it critically as it lay across her knee. "What's your trouble *now?*"

A faint wail had drifted down through the register from the room where Caroline was supposed to be asleep.

"All right. I'll get him for you." Garry laid aside her work to hunt round the room for the coon kitten, who, with the ingratitude of all cats towards those who seek to do them undesired kindness, had fled the warmth of Caroline's bed and was sitting with tucked-in paws as far under the sofa as he could squeeze. "That's the third time I've hauled that wretched kitten upstairs. Nothing will persuade Caroline that coon cats don't like being cuddled.

I hope the next time someone gives her a pet it'll be a tortoise; at least they can't run so fast.

"Do you know, Kay," she went on when they were settled once more, "I had an idea the other day. I don't know that it's brilliant, but it might work. Remember those funny pictures you used to make up for the kids when they were little—the Pilliwig family?"

"*Those* things?" Kay looked puzzled. "Martin used to like them. I haven't thought of them in years. I don't even remember how they went."

"I do. I'd remember Mrs. Pilliwig's hat and the way the little Pilliwigs looked if I lived to be a hundred. You used to make up the story and draw the pictures as you went along. Kay, I believe if you were to do a series of those any children's magazine in the world would want them."

"But they were just nonsense."

"Some of the best stuff in the world is nonsense," said Garry stoutly. "It's what everyone likes, anyway, and there's precious little of it that's any good. Those were fine just because they were nonsense and you weren't worrying about how they came out, but just went ahead and drew them."

"Wait a minute. I remember now I once made some on the back of another drawing."

[145]

Kay crossed the room to rummage through a portfolio of old sketches.

"It was when that little Cary girl came to tea. I wanted. . . Yes, here it is. It's about the zoo."

She smiled as she held out the paper for Garry to see. Garry was right. There was life and humor in the ridiculous little figures. There was more, too: a freedom of expression and a sure use of line that Kay didn't always get in her more studied drawings.

"See what I mean?"

"I don't know. I might be able to make something out of them if they were better drawn."

"There you go!" said Garry. "They don't want to be better drawn. They want to be just like you have them there."

"Eleven o'clock." Neal looked at his wrist watch. "What do you say we push on towards the ledges there and find a place to eat our sandwiches?"

They were halfway up the last rise of hillside. Below them there stretched a bare sparkling slope broken only by the track of their own footsteps and by a few gray bowlders thrusting here and there above the snow. Overhead the moon sailed in a sky dotted by tiny scudding clouds.

They had walked for miles, but Martin didn't even

feel tired. There was something in the pure keen air, the dazzle of moonlight on the snow, just the excitement of being out at night in an unfamiliar place, that went to his head like wine and made him feel wider awake, more alert to every sight and sound about him, than ever he had felt in the daytime. Everything looked strange and different. The patches of black shadow cast by bush or pasture wall stood out sharp and distinct; an old twisted wild-apple tree took fantastic shape in the moonlight, and the occasional faint lights of houses snuggled far down in the valley seemed to belong to another world.

So far they had seen one fox only. They were following an old wood road when he crossed their path unexpectedly in a clearing just ahead, a silent furtive shape that stood for a moment, head turned, and vanished. Jimmie had fired, but his hands shook with excitement and when the smoke cleared only some scattered pellet holes in the snow showed where the fox had stood.

"Passed clean through his fur and never touched him," Neal said, pointing to the marks. "Too bad!"

Across the shoulder of the hill now they could hear old Sam baying on another scent, two high-pitched notes, clear and mournful, like the sound of a bell at intervals on the frosty air. Neal listened.

"He's working round towards this way. We'll sit up there by the ledges and wait for him."

WINTERBOUND

They climbed the slope to a little plateau between flat outcropping ledges of granite. Neal found a sheltered hollow where they could sit, their backs to the rock and facing the open.

"See that big flat rock ledge straight in front of us?" he said. "When a fox is bein' hunted and he gets far enough ahead he'll always make for the highest place he can, so's he can take a good look round. Once you know that, and you know the country pretty well, you don't need to waste time followin' the hounds. You can get a good idea of which way they are workin' by listenin' to 'em, and then you go ahead and wait right where you know the fox is bound to come out. He'll be comin' up the other side of the hill now, and right there on that flat ledge is where he'll be likely to show himself, square against the skyline. He ain't in any hurry, no mor'n we are. We'll hear from old Sam when he's getting nearer."

He laid the gun down beside him and pulled the sandwiches out of his pocket.

"Guess some hot coffee'll taste good. You ain't cold, Martin?"

"Not a bit."

They ate their sandwiches and drank their coffee in turn from the little cup on the flask, talking in whispers. At intervals old Sam's voice reached them on the still air, sometimes nearer, sometimes further off.

[148]

GARRY'S JOB

"Workin' in a circle," Neal said. "He'll be another half hour, maybe."

Yesterday's wind had blown the loose snow from the ledges; in this sheltered angle it was warm and still. Martin finished his sandwich and leaned back against the flat slope of rock, his hands behind his head. Watching the moon as it fled in and out between the small fleecy clouds, rainbow hued in its halo, he felt as if the whole hillside were turning under him, and he sat up suddenly to find everything about him dizzy and strange. Neal laughed.

"That's the way folks get moon struck. When I was a kid mother was always telling me if I lay in the moonlight I'd go looney. That was one of her ideas, and the other was about night air being bad for you. Well, I managed to grow up in spite of both of 'em!"

The sandwiches were gone, the coffee finished. Neal racked his brain for hunting stories to while away the time as the minutes slowly passed. Jimmie was getting chilled and restless; he hated to keep still for long at a stretch and his missed shot earlier in the evening still rankled. He shifted his position several times to peer about, fidgeted here and there, and finally settled down again facing the other two, the .22 always ready in his hands. For a long time old Sam had been silent.

Suddenly, in the middle of a sentence, Neal's voice

[149]

paused. He made a movement towards his gun, then drew his hand noiselessly back, and instead his fingers tightened on Martin's arm beside him. Martin looked up.

There on the flat rock just above and behind Jimmie's head stood the fox. Unseen he had crept round behind them and now he was so near that Jimmie, had he known it, could have put out a hand and touched him. Martin could see the drawn-back silent snarl of his lips, the fixed eyes staring. Every hair of his coat stood out sharp and electric like spun glass in the moonlight. For what seemed a full minute he stood there motionless, one paw lifted, while Martin scarcely dared draw breath. Then Jimmie turned his head; the spell was broken. There was a blur and a flurry on the snow, something whipped past them like a flash of color and was gone. Neal rose to his feet, but it was too late.

"What a shot! Oh boy, what a shot!"

"Where—where?" Jimmie clutched at his rifle, staring wildly round.

"Right back of your head! I could have got him easy, but I wouldn't have risked it. Just sneaked up on us from round those bowlders, and us sittin' here all the time. Well, he got the laugh on us this time, I reckon."

A moment later old Sam loped up to them, puzzled and disappointed, to stare from one to the other and then thrust his black muzzle reproachfully into Neal's hand.

"No more hunting tonight," said Neal cheerfully, shouldering his gun. "That's settled it, hey, Sam? Don't know about you boys, but I'm just about chilled through all of a sudden. Guess we'll make tracks for home, and better luck next time."

It was as Neal said. For the first time Martin felt suddenly chilled and stiff. The excitement of the evening had dropped from him; drowsiness was creeping through his limbs. There was still a long walk before them, and by the time they had crossed the last stone wall into the pasture and saw the lighted kitchen window shining through the dusk he was ready to drop with sleep.

As he closed his eyes that night he seemed to see again, like a picture flashed on darkness, that swift moonlit vision of the fox in the snow.

VIII

On the Crooked Esses

GARRY came in bare headed from the mailbox, two bulky envelopes in her hand.

"Seed catalogues already. Didn't I tell you it smelled like spring today?" She paused by the drawing board where Kay sat sharpening pencils with a critical air. "You going to be busy working? I thought I'd go for a walk."

"Fine."

With Garry a walk meant a walk. Every once in so often she felt the need to get out alone in the open air and work off her accumulated energy in a long cross-country tramp.

The snow had almost gone—for the time being any-way. Only February, but there was a new blueness in the air, the ground felt elastic underfoot, and runnels of water trickled again in the roadside ditches. Willow shoots were already showing a trace of gold. In the pasture the Rowe cows, turned out for exercise, stood sniffing the breeze, their coats rough and dingy after long weeks in the stable.

Garry set out briskly over the hill. She had planned to go as far as Flat Top, a walk she had taken once with Mary in the early fall. It was a good four and a half miles, past the sugar-maple grove and the old Sullivan house at the crossroads, then up a narrow back road through woods with only a few scattered houses here and there on the way. Snow still lay in patches in the hollows; where the ground had begun to thaw there were deep ruts of mud that made slow going, and it was almost sunset before she passed the last belt of trees and came out on the open wind-swept plateau that gave the hill its name. Time only for a few minutes rest and a hurried look at the view before her before she must turn back.

Three roads met on the top of the hill; it seemed to Garry that it was the right-hand fork she and Mary had taken last fall when they turned to come home. The leaves were still on the trees, then, and she remembered the blaze of red and yellow that had lined the path. Now everything looked different with ground and bushes bare; it was hard to recognize landmarks again, but it did seem, after she had been walking some ten minutes, that the road was a good deal steeper and narrower than she remembered. There were no houses on it, and she was sure they had passed a white-painted house not so very far down. Anyway if it wasn't the same road it led more or less in the right direction; it would bring her out somewhere at the foot of the mountain, and she pushed on, quickening her pace a little, for dusk was coming on and with sunset the air had turned suddenly sharp and cold.

There was no mistake about it now; she had never been on this road before. It took a sudden zigzag twist, and as she peered down she could see the hillside drop away in a series of steep ledges.

"Well, here goes," Garry thought. "Good thing I'm on foot and not in a car; no car could ever take that turn."

As she stood, looking about, there was a stir and a crash in the bushes, something leaped out to dash past her. A deer, and a big one too; she caught the white bobbing flash of its tail as it sped down and round the bend. A moment later she heard the clatter of shod hoofs on the road below, and the sound of a girl's voice.

"Scared the horse and no wonder," sprang to her mind as she ran hurriedly down, for there was no mistaking that sudden startled scraping of iron on stones. "What a place to bring a horse up anyway!"

Rounding the next corner she came upon them; a pretty bay with a white blaze on his forehead, pulling at the end of the reins as his rider, her feet braced in the middle of the road, tried desperately to hold him back. The girl turned a frightened face as Garry ran down— and with reason: if the horse went over the edge of the road he would plunge straight down the ledges to the foot of the mountain.

Garry caught at the reins, and together they pulled him to a standstill. She knew the rider at once; it was the girl she had seen from the window of the old house that day last fall. There was dirt on her scarlet coat and leather breeches, blood oozing from a deep scratch over one eye. She had taken a nasty fall but had kept hold of the reins, and the horse must have dragged her as he plunged.

They looked at one another and drew breath.

"A close call," said Garry. "I bet that deer scared him out of a year's growth! He must have run square into you."

"It looked as big as a church!" There was a little catch in her voice; she reached up to pat the horse's trembling neck. "I'm lucky you came. I couldn't have held him alone another second, and if I once stopped pulling he'd have backed over the edge."

"Good thing you fell off, or you'd both have gone." Garry glanced at the drop before them. "How did you get on this road in the first place?"

"We were following an old wood track and it came out right above here. It was getting late and I thought this would bring us down the hill all right."

"It pretty nearly did, at that!"

She admired the girl's pluck, for it had nearly been a nasty accident and it was only chance that Garry had arrived when she did. Probably this road was never traveled from one year's end to another. For the first time she felt glad she had missed her own way that afternoon.

"Are you hurt much?"

"Only bruised, I guess. Starlight slipped too, that's the only reason I managed to keep hold of him. It doesn't matter about me, but I'm scared he's strained a muscle somewhere, and he isn't my own horse, worse luck. I'm just staying with some friends for a few days, and they let me take him out." She ran a hand anxiously down the satiny sweat-marked leg. "See that? It isn't much, but it'll stiffen up with the cold. I guess I'll have to begin walking him before it does."

Garry helped to brush her off, wiped the blood that had dried on her forehead, and together they began to lead the horse down hill. He set his feet cautiously, limping a little at each step.

"My name's Jane Bassett."

"Mine's Margaret Ellis, but they call me Garry."

"I like that. The worst of my name is that you can't do anything with it; it's too short. Have you any idea where this road goes to?"

"Only vaguely. I was walking over Flat Top and I got onto it by mistake coming back. I suppose it leads somewhere, but it doesn't look as if anyone ever used it, and I don't blame them."

"It's for all the world like a letter S, only crookeder."

Garry stopped short. Suddenly it came to her mind—the Crooked Esses. Neal had spoken once of a place called the Crooked Esses, somewhere the other side of Flat Top. But if this was it, she must be miles out of her way.

"I believe I do know, now," she said. "Your saying that made me think of it. Neal Rowe was telling us once. It used to be an old wagon road, and it ought to come out somewhere near a place called East Warley. But if it's the one I'm thinking of it gets a lot worse further on."

"We'll take a chance on it anyhow. East Warley is near where I'm staying." Jane took a fresh grip on the bridle, trying to conceal the fact that she was limping more than a little herself.

"Couldn't you ride if I give you a hand up?"

"It would put too much weight on him. I don't mind walking. But I'm awfully glad you came along. I'd hate

[158]

CROOKED ESSES

to be in a fix like this all alone, and not knowing the country. Whereabouts do you live?"

Garry told her.

"My brother has just got a place right near there. We haven't moved in yet; there's a lot to be done to the house first, but I expect we'll be up there this spring. We'll be neighbors—isn't that grand?"

"I know." Garry laughed. "You see, we're the people he rented the little house to."

"You . . . ? Why on earth didn't he tell me! He just said there was a family there but he never told me a word about them."

"We never even met him. Mother took the house through an agent. But I did see you once before." And Garry told her about the time she had been so nearly trapped in the old house. She left out the overheard conversation but made an amusing story of her ignominious escape over the woodshed roof and of Suzanne's scandalized face below. Jane was eager to hear more about the family and Garry had to give her a brief picture of Kay and Martin and Caroline, of their Christmas and the time they had during the cold spell, ending up with her own adventure at Roadside Nurseries, feeling that since Jane was so inclined to be friendly she might as well know the worst, as Kay would have called it, right from the beginning.

[159]

It was growing darker every minute. Garry had hoped to reach the bottom of the hill before the winter dusk shut in entirely, but already the daylight had gone. The road sloped more steeply at every turn. Here and there it was washed out in places and they had to pick their way across fissures and over loose rocks. Worst of all, a thin skim ice was beginning to form after the day's thaw, making it hard to keep one's footing.

Presently they came to a halt altogether, and even Garry looked dismayed. It was as though the road in front dropped away entirely, leaving only dark space before them.

"Looks like a bad bit," she said doubtfully. "You wait here while I go on ahead a little way and see what it's like."

She walked on cautiously, feeling her way foot by foot. The road was there all right, but it took a steep corkscrew turn that felt more like a staircase than a road. By daylight it mightn't have been so bad, but in this blackness one had to trust to luck for the next step.

"If the worst comes to the worst we can sit down and slide," she thought, prospecting a few paces further before turning back to where Jane stood waiting by the shivering horse.

"It's pretty steep, but I think we can get him down it."

CROOKED ESSES

They took hold of the bridle, one on each side, but for all their coaxing Starlight now refused to budge. He had seen what lay ahead and he didn't trust it, and the icy skim underfoot was making him increasingly nervous.

"Tell you what we'll do." Garry might not know much about horses but she generally found some inspiration in emergencies. "It's the slippery ground that worries him. We'll tie something over his feet so he can get a better grip."

Right then was the moment when a good old-fashioned petticoat would have come in useful, she decided, glancing down at her shabby corduroy breeches and woolen socks, while Jane feeling in the pockets of her own smart red jacket could only produce a silk handkerchief, so small and wispy that it set them both giggling as she pulled it out.

"Wait a minute." Garry stripped off windbreaker and sweater and began tugging at the faded hickory shirt she wore underneath.

"You can't—you'll catch cold!"

"No I won't." She set a foot on one sleeve and gave a yank, tearing the stuff neatly from neck to hem. "We'll tie it over his front hoofs and see how it works."

It was a bungling job but they managed somehow. "Patent non-skids!" said Garry as she tied the last knot. "Now, old boy, let's see how you like it."

WINTERBOUND

Starlight didn't like it at all, but after some pawing and fidgeting he found he could at least set hoof to the ground now without slithering, and little by little they coaxed him down the slope. It proved to be the steepest zigzag and the last; at the bottom they struck level ground and the worst of their troubles were over, though not all. The road continued a short distance only to lose itself in a grass-grown track that seemed to lead presently through a swamp, for they could feel rather than see the half-rotted planks that had been laid underfoot across the worst places. Here in the hollow it was blacker than ever; more than once they thought they had lost the narrow track entirely. Jane's riding boots, never meant for walking, had blistered her heel so that every step produced a raw twinge, and Garry had gone ankle-deep through skim ice into the thick mud. They had to fight their way through undergrowth that closed in on either side and as Garry pushed the stiff bushes apart she exclaimed: "I'll say no one has been over this road in years! It's worse than the jungle."

"Don't you ever have a moon up here?" Jane wailed.

"Not when you want it you don't. It's due to rise tonight about two-thirty. We might see it yet!" She was thinking of Kay, probably worried to death at home.

At last the track widened. They came out on a gravel road and saw lights in the distance—East Warley.

CROOKED ESSES

In the little general store, smelling of cheese and bacon and hot stove, Jane ran to the telephone while Garry talked to the storekeeper, who looked surprised to see the two scratched and muddy figures that burst in upon him, blinking at the light.

"East Warley. That's seven miles from home," she said. "Guess I'll call Kay up if you're through."

"They're sending a car right over for me," Jane told her. "We can drive you home first. Heavens, but I'm hungry!" She looked at her wrist watch for the first time. "Do you know that we were two hours and a half coming down that road?"

She found change in her pockets, and they bought crackers and cheese and chocolate, and ate them sitting by the stove while they waited. The house where Jane was staying was not very far off; it seemed only a few minutes before they heard the crunch of tires outside. A groom took charge of Starlight, who had been sheltered in the wagon shed behind the store, and the two girls climbed into the station wagon.

After that long slow walk it felt strange to be spinning so swiftly through the darkness.

"Drop me just at the turn of the road by Roadside Nurseries," said Garry. "I'll walk up the hill."

Jane protested, but Garry was firm. "It's only a short bit, and if I don't stretch my legs a little now I'll be all stiffened up. Thanks a lot, and remember the Crooked Esses!"

"As long as I live." Jane reached out a hand from the car. "So long. I've got to go back tomorrow, worse luck, and I'm joining mother in Bermuda. But first chance I get I'll be over to see you, and don't forget it!"

Jane went back to the comfort of a steaming bath and tray dinner on the library sofa; Garry to lounge at ease in the armchair beside Big Bertha, while Martin pulled off her sodden shoes, Kay ran to make hot tea, and Caroline hunted and warmed her slippers.

"Heavens, you'd think I'd been to the North Pole," she grumbled, secretly pleased with these little attentions, since she was not usually the one to get them.

"We kept some supper in the oven for you," Caroline said, "but it got all dried up while we were busy worrying."

This announcement, so typical of the household, set everyone laughing, and Garry exclaimed: "Do you remember the time Penny and I took that long walk and got lost? All the way home we kept our spirits up thinking about supper, and when we got back the kitchen stove was cold and you were all out on the road hunting for us! Never mind; I ate up half the grocery store while we were waiting, so I'm all right this time."

CROOKED ESSES

"Tell me about this girl." Kay set the teapot down
and pulled her chair up to the stove.

"Nice, and no nonsense; you'll like her. If the rest of
the family are anything like she is we'll be lucky. Charles
sounds all right, even if he was snooty about renting the
house to us. There is a sister-in-law that's a pain in the
neck—bossy kind, but Jane seems to get along with her
all right. Maybe she won't be up here much; I think they
travel a lot, anyway, from what Jane told me." For the
half hour in the grocery store had covered quite a little
exchange of confidences. "It's going to seem strange with
other people living up here, after all this time with just
the Rowes and ourselves. I don't know whether I'll like it
or not."

She was thinking of the long quiet months when the
hillside seemed just to belong to them, two friendly
families hemmed round in their own little personal
world.

"I shall. It'll be a new place to visit," returned Caroline, who was naturally social-minded and foresaw pos-
sibilities. "I like seeing people and going places, and up
here there isn't anybody but just us'n the Rowes, and
all the girls at school live way off and if they did ask me
I couldn't ever go 'cause we haven't any car."

"Then you'd better learn to keep your hair brushed

[165]

and your stockings pulled up," Kay told her. "If you start practicing now you'll be all ready by spring."

Caroline looked ready to glower, but the smile in Kay's eyes made up for her words, and Garry added quickly:

"Cheer up, Caroline. Here's two strangers in my teacup this very minute, a great big fat one and a funny little thin one—see? Now shut your eyes and wish three times, and we'll see which of them comes true!"

IX

"Z. Y. 3."

KAY was working hard on the Pilliwig family. She showed nothing to Garry as yet, but the little sheaf of finished drawings laid away in the pine blanket chest where she kept her belongings was growing steadily. Easier to work now, too, when her fingers were no longer so stiffened by cold and it was possible to use her drawing table by the window instead of sitting hunched by the stove with a board on her knees. The first few attempts had been wooden and lifeless. In the beginning her mind seemed a complete blank, but by degrees the spirit of the thing took hold of her, new ideas cropped up, and the drawings gained in freedom as she began to find a real enjoyment in their invention.

Garry had started seed-flats indoors, and her precious boxes, covered with odd panes of glass, filled every available sunny window space upstairs and down. She watered and shifted, covered and uncovered, a dozen times a

day according to the temperature, and woe betide anyone who moved a box or carelessly opened a window at
the wrong moment. She had cauliflowers in the living
room and tomatoes on the shelf behind the kitchen stove,
and waged a continual war with the coon kitten, who took
a diabolic pleasure in scratching up the seeds the instant
her back was turned. In the intervals of caring for her
vegetable infants she found time to walk down the hill
and visit small Julia, seven weeks old now and fast out-
growing the clothes basket in which she slept proudly
under the peach-colored silk quilt. It was on her return
from one of these visits that Kay, deep in the weekly
letter from Santa Fé, waved a hand to a letter and a
postcard propped on the mantelshelf. The postcard was
a greeting from Jane, a view of Bermuda with a very
blue sea and a very white beach. The typewritten envelope was addressed to Miss Margaret Ellis and bore a
New York postmark.

Garry, opening it, gave a sudden whoop.

"You see—she's coming after all!"

"Who?" Kay looked up from her letter.

"That woman. The one we wrote to. She's coming
next week."

"Garry, you're fooling!"

"I'm not. Listen here." She read aloud:

"Z.Y.3."

"Dear Miss Ellis,

"I am sorry to have been so long answering your letter. If you still feel inclined to put me up I shall be very glad to come to you on the proposed terms, and will arrive on the afternoon train next Monday, the twenty-first. If by any chance you have altered your plans and find this no longer convenient, please wire me at above address.

"Yours very sincerely,

"EMILY HUMBOLD. (Z.Y.3.)

"Good for her!"

Kay looked scared. "I'd given up all idea of it. She'll find the place awful, Garry. We can't possibly let her come!"

"Try and stop her," Garry returned. "She sounds pretty businesslike about it, if you ask me. I like that. And she hasn't asked one single question either. I told you that letter would produce an effect!"

"Turned her brain, more likely, if she's read all you wrote her and still wants to try it out. We'll just have some sort of crank or lunatic on our hands and you'll have to deal with it all," said Kay with an air of washing her hands of the whole business. "I'll do my best, but I bet you she won't stay a week, once she finds out what it's really like."

"Well, that'll be fourteen dollars anyway, and if she doesn't stay we can always charge her for the month ahead, like that old devil of a Cummings did; no good having experiences if you don't learn something by them. I shall be the business and practical head of the family. All you need do is to be a pleasant dignified hostess and lend the right atmosphere. *And* help with the meals. Heaven knows I'm no cook. All they ever ate at the Collins's was fried potatoes and stew."

"Atmosphere!" Kay looked round at the room, littered with her own work, the rugging frame, temporarily neglected, leaning in one corner with a tangle of cut rags beside it, and Garry's seed-flats and boxes everywhere in evidence. "Do you suppose we'll ever get the place to look like anything again?"

"Leave it to me. I told her we were a busy family, and we might as well preserve the effect. Let's see: today's Thursday. We've got four whole days to fix up in."

"We'll need them," said Kay darkly.

Once the wire was sent—"Perfectly all right, will expect you Monday."—even Garry herself felt a little daunted, with a sensation of bridges definitely burned behind her. It would have been one thing for the unknown Z.Y.3 to have arrived during those first days when they were still all excited about the project; it was quite another to have her turning up now after all these weeks, a real and actual person. But having started the business Garry was determined to see it through all the same, and spent the next two days in a fury of sweeping and scrubbing, dragging unwanted articles up to the attic and carrying others down, till in the end Kay had to admit that the guest room at least looked presentable. Ever since Mrs. Cummings sternly shook its dust from her feet it had become mainly a glory hole for this and that. Cleared out now and tidied, with new curtains and the best bedspread (long known in the Ellis family as the White Elephant) carefully displayed, Kay's one finished rug on the floor and a fine old farmhouse pine table, one of Penny's auction weaknesses, set for a desk between window and fireplace with a bookshelf above it of Garry's contriving, it had quite a comfortable air.

"Thank heaven you didn't cut those old damask curtains up for rugs," Garry said. "I hung the faded part where it doesn't show, and the red makes the room look warmer. All the furniture's waxed, and a job it was, too. The White Elephant looks pretty awful, but it's brand new and it ought to impress her, and there isn't a thing else we could use; I hunted through every trunk up there. I hate frilly things myself."

The White Elephant, a flounced and billowy affair of

sea-green rayon taffeta, certainly seemed to have been
wafted by some strange mistake into its present setting.
The original motive power, as usual, had been Cousin
Carrie, on the occasion of "doing over" her own guest
room three years ago.

"It doesn't go with the rest. We never did have the
sort of room it belongs to, anyway. ("Thank God!"
Garry murmured.) You can bring down the hand-woven
cover off my bed and I'll use the extra army blanket instead." This was generous on Kay's part, but since Garry
had set the pace she felt bound to keep up with it. "We'll
bring in that small easy-chair from the living room;
she'll want something comfortable to sit in."

"A gentle hint to stay in her own quarters, you really
mean!"

"Well . . ." They both laughed, remembering Mrs.
Cummings and her trailing possessions. "How about
cushions? We could spare a few."

"To recline on in the intervals of composition. We
might get a few hints from Emily Post on furnishings for
the literary worker. I suppose she'll bring her own typewriter, but I did remember an ash tray!"

A good deal of joking went into the final preparations,
but as train time drew near they were beginning to feel a
little qualmish, especially Garry, who had undertaken to

do the honors. A kind of reverent hush descended on the household, relieved by occasional nervous giggles. Martin and Caroline looked unnaturally slick about the head and scrubbed about the face, and Caroline in particular kept up an aimless wandering about the room which drove her sisters to desperation.

"Can't you for goodness' sake act naturally instead of prowling like a panther in a cage?" Kay demanded. "Take a book and read. Play paper dolls. Do *something!*"

There was a smothered explosion from Martin, and Caroline retorted: "Well, you said not to get the room all mussed up, and all my books . . ."

" 'Let's be talking,' " quoted Garry, and her reminder of the nervous family in Dickens's pages, trying to appear at ease, set them all off so completely that Kay was still choking when they heard the car just outside.

"There she is!"

Garry, feeling the eyes of the assembled family on her back, strode to the breach. She could hear Edna's voice, cheery and conversational as she climbed out of the car, which was a relief; none of that disapproving silence which had shrouded Mrs. Cummings's arrival. Suitcases, typewriter, and rug bundle were handed out; Garry was just hurrying down the front path when a volley of

soprano yelps, issuing apparently from the very bosom
of the tweed-coated figure coming to meet her, made her
jump. A deep voice said:

"Shut up, Arabella, this instant. Don't be such a little
fool.—Are you Miss Margaret Ellis?"

"I'm so glad you came. Pretty cold still, isn't it? Hello,
Edna!"

Garry's prepared speech had forsaken her. They shook
hands—a hearty grip—and in the glare of the car lights
she saw thrusting from Miss Emily Humbold's broad
chest a tiny head, the size and color of a small russet
orange, with two wrathful eyes glaring from a ruff of
tawny fur. Arabella.

"She won't bite; she just enjoys being disagreeable,
that's all." Miss Humbold picked up the larger of the
two suitcases and followed Garry indoors.

"My sister Kay, Miss Humbold. And Martin and
Caroline." Garry hoped her voice didn't sound as nerv-
ous as she felt, for introductions always muddled her
and just now she was feeling anything but the competent
"Miss Ellis" who had composed that famous letter. But
Kay came to her rescue.

"I do hope you had a comfortable journey up. Would
you like to take your things off or sit down and get warm
first?"

Miss Humbold pulled off her hat—a plain sensible

[174]

hat with no nonsense about it. Very like its owner, Garry decided instantly, after one look at the square face, short grizzled hair, and keen eyes.

"Splendid, thank you. We came over the bumps in fine style. Where's my nice taxi lady, by the way? I owe her money, which isn't so important, and a great deal of gratitude which is. She rescued me from a pink-eyed young man who seemed to have no idea who you were or where you lived, but insisted on trying to take me there just the same."

"That was Eddie Cregan," Edna said, bringing in the luggage. "I guess he don't know much about the roads this side of town. He don't know much about anything as a matter of fact, but that never stops him." She carried the remaining bags through to the bedroom, "That'll be two dollars, so long as you're staying with the Ellises here, and I won't charge you nothing extra for the bumps!"

"Can't you stay a minute?" This from Garry.

"Mm-mm. I got to get back." Edna always kept business and pleasure strictly separate. She nodded to Martin, rumpled Caroline's carefully slicked hair in passing, and added to her late client: "Don't you go letting that Saint Bernard loose till I get safe in the car, now!"

As the door closed behind her Miss Humbold exclaimed: "I don't know when I've enjoyed a drive so much!" A remark which established her credit immediately in the Ellis family.

The parlor bedroom looked cozy with red curtains drawn and a fire on the open hearth. Kay and Garry had taken a lots of pains with it—pains that were not wasted, as they could see by the pleased look on their guest's face.

"It's just what I like: a room you can work and be comfortable in, and no frills. And that open fire is grand!"

"We've got a small stove, but we thought you'd rather have it this way. And there's all the wood you want for burning. Supper will be ready in just a few minutes, and I'll bring you some hot water." Garry cast an anxious glance at the room's one blot, in her opinion—a little painted washstand tucked away in one corner. "We wanted to give you a screen for that, but there's not one in the house. Maybe I could fix something else. I guess I warned you this was real country, and all we have is a tin bathtub!"

"I hoped I was going to wash at the pump, from your letter."

"Not this weather!" Garry laughed and Caroline, hanging in the background, gave a smothered snicker.

"Well, it wouldn't be the first time," said Miss Humbold cheerfully. "Anyway it's all nonsense, washing in the country. What I like is a little healthy dirt; not city dirt, but the kind that goes with outdoors and a good country appetite. Which reminds me, I'd better feed Arabella now, and then she'll be more settled."

The tiny Pomeranian was sidling about the floor uneasily. Her small nose worked; her round eyes that seemed just on the brink of tears were fixed imploringly on her mistress, her slender legs, no thicker than a pencil, trembled with suspicion. Garry stooped to put out a hand, but at her movement there was a startling transformation. The thin legs stiffened, Arabella's ears went back and she gave a sharp venomous growl like the warning of a rattlesnake.

"Don't mind her; she's apt to go off like an alarm clock that way. Just pay no attention to her and she'll be all right," Miss Humbold said.

Supper was an easier and more informal meal than any of them had expected. Even Caroline, who had good behavior written all over her, sat at first with her hands in her lap and only lifted her eyes to say "please" and "thank you," began to unbend; Martin got past the yes-and-no stage and found himself talking naturally, and Garry felt the weight of responsibility dropping rapidly from her shoulders.

"You see," she said to Kay over the dishwashing, while Miss Humbold was unpacking, "she's nice. We're going to get along all right."

"A good beginning, if we can manage to keep it up. How was the supper?" For that had been Kay's anxiety.

"Fine!"

Tapping at the door later, to make sure their guest had everything needed for the night, Garry found her stretched comfortably in the armchair, her feet to the fire and an open book on her knee. A blue eiderdown lay across the foot of the bed and from a dent in its fold Arabella's sharp little eyes peered out, a faint sleepy growl sounded no louder than a sigh.

Evidently Arabella, too, was at home.

There are some people who seem able to settle into a household without, as Garry put it, causing a single ripple. Miss Emily Humbold was one of them. She asked no questions, she had an amazing knack of knowing where everything was without being told, she went her own way and expected the rest of the family to go theirs. She slept late, breakfasted in her room, and sometimes they saw scarcely anything of her till supper time. Long after the girls had gone to bed at night they could still hear the brisk tapping of her typewriter in the room below.

"Z.Y.3."

Her habits fascinated Caroline, who had been told beforehand that Miss Humbold was a writer, and that writers were never under any circumstances to be disturbed at work. Passing the open door one day she saw Miss Humbold, cigarette in hand, engaged in pacing up and down the floor, and stood staring at her in open curiosity.

"Kay said you were busy writing a book."

"I am," said Miss Humbold, pausing.

"Is that how you do it?"

"It's how I do most of it."

"Goodness, I should think you'd get tired. I should think . . ."

"Caroline!" Kay's voice sounded a warning from the kitchen, but Caroline only gave a little wriggle.

"I should think it would be lots easier if you sat down."

"I have tried that," said Miss Humbold, "but it doesn't work nearly as well. You see, everybody has their own way of doing things. I like to write walking up and down, but sometimes in town that's a nuisance to other people, so that's why I wanted to come to the country. Country floor boards are so much stronger."

Caroline looked from the solid wide flooring to Miss Humbold's even more solid figure, and decided that Miss Humbold was probably right.

"Do you s'pose you'll get it finished soon? I just keep

hoping you won't 'cause Garry says when you do you'll go back to the city again, and I don't want you to."

Miss Humbold's booming laughter rang out.

"I tell you one thing," she said, nodding confidentially, "but don't you go telling anyone else. It's going to be a mighty funny book if I ever do get it finished!"

In spite of her peculiar methods of book writing Miss Humbold was a person after Caroline's own heart. She liked going for walks, and whenever possible she took Caroline and Shirley with her. She had a way of talking nonsense with such solemnity that the little girls were never quite sure how far to believe her, but when it came to serious matters she took a profound interest in everything, liked to discuss a question from every possible angle, and could out-argue even Caroline herself.

Arabella was less adaptable. She still flitted noiselessly about the house, reserved and dignified, resisting all approaches. Her one object in life was to guard Miss Humbold in a world beset, according to Arabella, with incalculable dangers.

Neal always affected terror when he caught sight of her pattering at Miss Humbold's heels. "You watch that bloodhound of yours," he would call. "I'm scared she's goin' to tear my old Sam to pieces if she once gets a sight of him. We ain't none of us safe with a savage animal like that roamin' the country!"

And when he dropped in at the house he would first poke his head cautiously round the door. "You sure you got that bloodhound chained safe?"

"That little thing's got me beat," he admitted to Miss Humbold one evening when they were all gathered round the stove in the Rowes' kitchen, Arabella as usual on her mistress's knee. "It isn't often I can't make friends with a dog, but she won't have a word to say to you. She's no bigger'n a ball of knittin' wool but she's got the spirit of a dog ten times her size, and I bet you if she ever was scared of anything she'd be too proud to let on!"

It was Garry who first succeeded in making friends with her, and that by accident.

From the beginning Arabella and the coon cat had been at daggers drawn. In the house there was no chance of trouble, but on this morning Miss Humbold was at work and Arabella had wandered out by herself. Usually she kept close to the house, but there was something to-day in the sunshine and the smell of the air tempting to a small dog and she forgot her caution. It was the chance for which the coon cat had been waiting.

Both he and the Rowes' old tomcat were out in the field below the house, watching each other at a distance as cats will, for there was no love lost between the two of them, but at the sight of Arabella all differences were forgotten: here was a common enemy. They exchanged glances, and each began to stroll forward, stalking her. Arabella saw them. It was an awful moment for a little dog. Her tail drooped; slowly and with dignity she turned round and prepared to retreat.

Garry, coming round the corner of the house, was just in time to see her headed for the stone steps leading up to the terrace, the two cats bearing down upon her, one on either side, with a businesslike air. Arabella, brought up in an apartment, managed stairs with great difficulty. These were high and steep and they must have loomed to her like a mountain. Painfully but proudly she made the ascent step by step, her head held high, never once looking behind her, and it was not until she reached the top that Garry saw actual tears rolling down her cheeks.

She held out her arms and for the first time Arabella sprang into them, burying her little nose in Garry's neck. The ice was finally broken.

X

Company

WITH spring in the offing the days passed quickly. There were still occasional flurries of snow that lay for a few hours and melted again—"poor man's manure" Neal called it, welcoming the good it did to the fields— but in the damp hollows skunk cabbage was already uncurling, song sparrows were singing in the leafless boughs of the apple trees and every sugar maple along the roadside bore its hanging sap pail. Year after year Mary Rowe declared that she wouldn't be bothered with syrup-making, but every spring she gave in, and it was the children's task after they got home from school to make the rounds of the scattered trees by fence and wood lot, empty the little sap buckets into a big milk pail, and carry the clear watery sap back to be dumped into the flat sugaring-pan over the outdoor fireplace. Twenty gallons to a gallon of syrup, Mary reckoned, and that meant a good many trips back and forth.

Feeling like millionaires with Emily Humbold's

[183]

fourteen dollars a week rolling in steadily, Kay and Garry had ordered paint and wall papers from the mail-order catalogue, and for days past the house had been turned upside down, to the horror of Arabella and the coon cat who both loathed the pervading smell of turpentine. The hated drab of the living-room woodwork had given place to a soft pinkish lilac that suited the pale yellow walls, and a deeper shade of pumpkin yellow was chosen for kitchen and pantry. Wall papers had taken longer to decide upon, for most of the patterns were either too elaborate or too modern for Kay's taste, but they found at last a tiny sprig pattern for Penny's bedroom, a rosebud chintz for Caroline who liked gay color, and an old-fashioned trellis design in brown on a light background that just suited their own room. Papering had to wait for warmer weather but the painting was almost done, and Kay was counting the days until Bertha, her winter's duties nobly ended, could be dismantled and carried out piecemeal to the woodshed and the room begin to look at last as it should.

Kay had thrown herself into the job with energy, glad of something to take her mind off her own problems. The Pilliwigs were finished. They had already gone to two publishers and come promptly back again, and Kay was beginning to feel the old hopelessness about trying to do anything from this small corner of the world. Stamps cost money; she was all for giving up and putting the drawings aside, but Garry was insistent and she had sent them off again now for the third time, with no greater hopes of success. Meanwhile the house was something she could give her mind to at least, and with more rewarding effect.

The color in the living room was all right, she decided, touching the mantel shelf gingerly with a finger to see if yesterday's final coat was dry. It was a queer shade; there had been an awful moment when neither she nor Garry felt quite sure about it, but in the end it proved exactly what she wanted, something that took warm tones in the shadow and seemed to change in color with the changes of light in the room.

One more coat to the pantry shelves, and then everything would be fairly straight. She pulled on her rubber gloves, picked out the yellow paint brush, and set to work.

Emily Humbold, driven from her typewriter not so much by the smell of paint as by what she called one of her "woolly spells," which overtook her every so often, had spent the morning happily trundling manure in a wheelbarrow from the Rowes' barnyard to the new flower border which Garry was making on the south side of the house. If anyone had told the Ellises a month ago that their literary paying guest would spend her free time wheeling manure or shifting rocks they would have been much surprised. But it was Emily who had marched over to borrow the wheelbarrow that morning, and would relinquish it to no one; it was Emily who had dragged or excavated most of the big rocks to finish the terrace that Garry had begun last year.

"My parents made a big mistake sending me to college," she said one day. "They should have brought me up to be a road maker or a stone mason. Think of all this solid bone and muscle going to waste!"

It didn't go to waste here, for there was plenty of use for it. With Emily Humbold on one end of a crowbar, even the most stubborn rock was bound to yield.

She sat on the empty wheelbarrow now, a sturdy figure in her short tweed skirt and gray sweater, watching Garry dig. The smell of burning brush drifted over from across the road where Neal too was making ready for spring.

A gray roadster, coming up the hill, slowed up by the bars and stopped, and Garry turned her head just in time to see a young man bearing down upon them, waving his hat.

"Is it Emily, or do my eyes deceive me? Emily, of all people, and having a thoroughly good time as usual!"

Arabella crouched under the wheelbarrow, broke into a volley of barking, and Miss Humbold picked her up before she turned a calm face on the visitor.

COMPANY

"Our absentee landlord. Well, well!"

She held out a broad grimy paw across Arabella's head and added to Garry: "This is my nephew Charles, in case you never met him. I believe he owns another small neglected property somewhere up the road."

Garry felt her cheeks burn, remembering the last occasion when she had seen this same Charles, and wondering if Jane had told him about it.

"I never knew . . ."

"No, it isn't a thing one would boast about," Emily put in. "I daresay you never expected to see me up here, did you?"

"One can expect to see you anywhere," Charles retorted, sitting on the edge of the wheelbarrow beside her. "The last time I saw you was two years ago. You were on all fours, crawling out of a cave somewhere in the Ozark Mountains. Never shall I forget that vision! So when I spotted you just now—what brought you up here anyway?"

"Nothing to do with you, so you needn't get so suspicious. I came on the perfectly good invitation of some nice people whom I had never even met, and I'm having the time of my life."

"So I see. Well, I hope they're beginning to know by now just what they've let themselves in for!" He smiled at Garry. "A visit from my Aunt Emily is rather like an earthquake; you're never quite the same again. I've known people who actually barricade their doors when they see her coming."

"An Ellis fears nothing," said Emily loftily. "That's one reason why we get along together so well." She rose, brushing the earth from her skirt. "Don't for heaven's sake go telling the rest of the family where I am, now. I came up here to collect my scattered brains and have a quiet place to work in, which only shows that one can never hope to get away with anything in this world. Since you don't seem to have troubled to meet your tenants before, you might as well come in now and get it all over with."

She linked her arm in her nephew's and marched him up to the house, while Garry flew round behind the woodshed to poke her head through the kitchen window and warn Kay of their unexpected caller. The kitchen was a mess; saucepans and dishes piled haphazard on floor and table together with all the other contents of the pantry, including half a cold ham and the remains of yesterday's stew in a soup tureen, while Kay, in a paint-smeared smock and with a blue handkerchief tied over her head, stood putting the last touches on the pantry shelves. Garry, not wanting to raise her voice, went through a mysterious pantomime, her head framed in the open window, and Kay was just exclaiming: "For heaven's

COMPANY

sake can't you *say* what you want!" when Emily and
Charles appeared on the threshold.

Garry ducked promptly, leaving Kay to pick her way
across the household chattels.

"I'm afraid we're in an awful mess; won't you go
through to the living room and I'll be right in."

She dragged her gloves off, not sure from Garry's
pantomime and this sudden descent of their landlord
(for Garry had managed to convey that much) whether
he hadn't come to demand the house back at a week's
notice and racking her brains guiltily to remember if she
had sent off last month's rent check on the proper day.
Emily Humbold meantime was enjoying the situation;
it was a chance to pay off some old scores against this
nephew who always made fun of her, and she forced
Charles to admit that he had never set foot in the little
house before, except on the first day he came to look
over the property, and that it was no thanks to him,
as she sternly put it, that the walls hadn't crumbled and
the roof fallen in on his tenants' heads.

"You're just typical of all these property owners who
disgrace the housing situation in this country," she
boomed at him. "You rent places out without taking the
slightest interest in their upkeep. Come on, Garry; while
we've got him here you'd better show him all the cracks
you had to stuff up this winter, and all the places where

the roof leaks. And how about that kitchen pump, while we're at it?"

"You just shut up; you're as bad as Arabella, every bit!" Charles told her. "Miss Ellis, I hope you weren't too awfully uncomfortable this winter. I left everything to the agent, but I had meant to come up here myself some time and make sure."

There was a great difference between the house as he had seen it on that first visit, with unscraped walls and smoky ceilings, the dust and litter of its last occupancy still strewing the floors, and the way it looked now. Kay got over her first shyness as she showed him what they had done, and in a few minutes they were deep in the discussion of beams and floor boards, Dutch ovens and old pine paneling, for this was something about which she felt thoroughly at home and could talk freely.

Garry beckoned Emily out into the kitchen, and pulled the door to.

"You never told us about Mr. Bassett being your nephew, all this time."

Emily Humbold smiled, for there was something accusing in Garry's voice.

"Listen, young woman. I'll tell you exactly how the whole thing happened. When I got your letter I liked it. Out of nearly fifty answers it was the only one that was frank and sensible and friendly, and with a sense of humor, too. But it reached me late. I'd already taken a room for a month in a farmhouse up in New York state and your letter was forwarded on to me there. I put it aside and I thought maybe I'd write to you anyway; I wish now I had. Then . . ." she paused a second, "I happened to be spending the week-end with some friends in East Warley the same time that Jane was there. She told me what happened on that ride she took. And that settled me. I put two and two together and I went straight back and packed up my things, and I wrote to you the week after. I wasn't going to tell you all this, but as things have happened I might just as well. I heard Charles had bought a house somewhere out this way, but until Jane told me about your helping her that afternoon and who you were I'd never connected your letter with this place at all."

"It wasn't anything. It just happened we both got lost on the same road, and if it wasn't for her horse getting scared we might never have met at all."

"I suppose Jane never told you that she'd taken a turn of the rein round her wrist, like the young idiot she is, and that with the horse dragging that way she couldn't have let go if she'd wanted to? Well, think it over. I happen to be rather fond of Jane."

"So that was it. I thought she looked scared." Garry was sober, remembering that drop of the ledges and

Jane's face when she first caught up with her. "No, she never told me that."

"She wouldn't. You and I and Jane are the only ones that know it now. Charles would have given her the devil, for she's ridden enough to have more sense, but I guess all he'll ever know is that she lost her way and you helped her home. We'll leave it at that. Only I did want you to know some time how I felt about it."

Garry looked at the kitchen clock, perched temporarily on the bread box. "How about some lunch?"

"Can we do it?"

"I guess so. There's cold ham and potato salad, and we'll have something hot to drink with it if I can ever get at the stove again!" Garry laughed. "Take him off for a walk, and Kay and I will fix things. I didn't mean to act mad, and it was just my darn pride anyway, for I spent one whole evening composing that letter and I did think I'd turned out a masterpiece, though Kay swore you'd never want to come once you'd read it!"

"Little she knew me!" Emily retorted.

As they strolled up the hill towards the Bassett house Emily said to her nephew:

"I hope you realize those young people did every bit of the work on that place themselves, and that they spent their own earnings buying the paint and wall paper. You can see for yourself what they've made of it. That eldest girl has a real feeling for line and arrangement, and her taste is instinctive, though she hasn't much experience. You might do worse than let her have a hand in experimenting with your place. She's restless and ambitious, but she puts her whole heart in anything she undertakes, and though she's all for painting just now I think she'd do a great deal better in work of this kind, if she had a chance to find it out for herself."

"She's done a nice job there, and she knows quite a lot; I found that out. I did feel a bit ashamed, but when I told the agent to let the house to year-round tenants I was thinking of local people, and how could I know it would be anyone like this? How about the rest of the family?"

"The father is an archæologist, away on a two-year expedition. The mother is in New Mexico at this minute, taking care of some sick relative. The girls undertook to manage for themselves this winter, and they have certainly done it."

"How did you come into the picture?"

"Through advertising for a place to board—the kind I wanted. Garry saw the ad and answered it, and I wish you'd seen her letter. I'll show it to you some day. Sort of 'I'll tell you the worst, and if you still like it you can take a chance.'" Emily chuckled. "I decided a young woman with that much sense was worth knowing. They've turned the house upside down for my comfort, I pay them fourteen dollars a week and they're scared that's too much."

"That the red-headed one?" Charles asked.

"She's the business head of the family, and a lot more too. She's keen on gardening and wants to go in for it practically—take a job with some nurseries down the road, if she can get it. She might, for she isn't afraid of work, or of anything else for that matter."

"She'd be a nice friend for Jane. They're about the same age."

"I thought of that, too," said Emily innocently.

Lunch was all ready when they returned, with a transformed Kay as hostess, and after there was another visit to the big house, Emily this time staying at home to work, as she said, but actually feeling that the three young people would get on more easily alone.

Garry, entering respectably through the front door this time, wandered off by herself to explore the upper rooms once more, leaving Charles and Kay below. It was the first time Kay had set foot in the house and nothing could drag her at first from the big living room with its lovely old paneling and perfect proportions, nor the entry with its graceful curving stair rail and wide fanlight above the door. Sagging floors, crumbling plaster, meant nothing to her, for the gracious spirit of the old house still survived its years of neglect and disrepair, and her quick eyes saw only the beauty that care and money could so easily restore.

"When I first saw this one room," Charles told her, "I knew I wanted the place. I didn't care what the rest of it was like. Half the family still think I'm crazy, for there's a fortune to be spent on it that I haven't even got and it may be years before we get all the work done. My mother hasn't seen it yet, but I can count on her; she feels the way I do about old places, and Jane is happy anywhere in the country."

"When will you start work on it?"

"As soon as possible. I'm going to talk to Neal Rowe. He's a good workman and he knows a lot about old houses. He's lived in this part of the country all his life, and if I put him in charge I can trust to things being done the way I want them. I shall be here off and on myself, and as soon as the place is habitable I hope to move into it, even if it means camping at first."

Charles had to leave early for the long drive back to town, but not until he had had his talk with Neal, and Garry could hardly wait till supper was cleared before flying across the road to learn the result, for she knew what a job like this would mean to the Rowe family.

"Did you hear the news?" Neal greeted her. "If the old truck was working I'd go down the hill this minute and buy ice cream for the crowd."

"Is it really settled? Hurrah!"

Neal nodded. "Steady work for pretty near the whole summer. Tuesday he'll be back, and we're to go over the place together. He wants me to hire the men and look after the whole job for him. I told him I knew every inch of that house inside and out, for an uncle of mine farmed the place for five years when I was a kid. There's two closed-up fireplaces in the upper rooms there he never even knew about. We'll start work next week if the weather holds up. How about me hiring you, Garry, just for a beginning? Want to get up on the roof there and start ripping shingles? That's a nice easy job that should just about suit you!"

"Fine with me, but you'd better get Emily on it. She'd be a grand hand."

Neal laughed.

"Emily? We won't be able to keep Emily off it, not if I know her. She as good as offered yesterday to do my spring plowing for me. Said she'd always had a hankering to hold a plow handle and feel what it was like. Maybe I'll let her try it out yet."

"She'd make a good job of it, too," Mary defended.

COMPANY

"Believe me, anything that Emily Humbold undertook to do, she'd do it and do it well, and don't you make any mistake!"

The old truck was put into working order forthwith— Neal was already promising himself a new one before the summer was out—and in the next week or so it made many trips up and down the hill, where the gray roadster, too, was by now a familiar visitor. Then came the spring thaw, when the deep frost was slowly working itself out of the ground and for ten days the hill was axle-deep in mud. Cars could go neither up nor down, and the two households were almost as completely shut off from the world as they were by the winter snows. Mail was left on the lower road to be fetched by the children, who picked their way along the fence banks and floundered in rubber boots through a sea of yellow mire to reach the school bus. Mud and more mud, but the pasture was turning greener day by day, pussy willows were out in the swamps, and Mary Rowe, standing at her open kitchen window, was sure she had heard the first robin in the apple orchard.

A letter from Santa Fé. In a few weeks now Penny would be coming home.

☆ ✩ XI ✩ ☆

Ready for Penny

EVERY day now the sound of hammers rang busily on the air, where Neal and his helpers were at work on the big house. The old ragged shingles were gone—without Emily's help—and already the new roof showed raw and bright above the thickening tree tops. A regular eyesore, Garry thought as she looked across every morning from the kitchen window, though time and weather would soon tone it down to the familiar gray that she loved. But she liked the smell of new lumber, the sounds of work and activity that seemed as much a part of spring as the call of robins or the blue gleam of the little Quaker ladies dotting the pasture slope.

Charles Bassett managed to spend a good part of his time on the hillside, staying at the Rowes and only driving back to town for occasional trips. They saw a good deal of him at the little house, for scarcely a day passed that he did not drag Kay off with him to consult about one thing or another in connection with the work.

It was after one of these brief absences in town that he brought his brother and sister-in-law up with him to see the alterations, and Garry's early opinion of Gina changed when she came upon her sitting under the Rowes' apple trees making dandelion chains for Tommy, with Caroline and Shirley one on either side.

"I like her," Caroline said after the car had driven off. "I wish she was going to live here all the time."

"I guess her bark's worse than her bite, after all," Garry admitted to Kay that evening, and was a little surprised to have her sister turn on her roundly.

"I don't see where you ever got that idea of her in the first place. I think she's awfully nice and very friendly. Foreigners may strike you as different, but that's only because you haven't met very many, or the right kind, before. You do make up your mind in such queer ways about people before you even know anything about them, and it's a great mistake!"

Garry took the rebuke meekly; not for worlds would she have told her sister where that particular idea did come from, and she was gladder than ever now that she had kept her own council at the time.

"You know, Garry," Kay went on, setting the supper tumblers in an even row as she dried them, "I think it would do you a world of good if you took a little trouble to be friendly with the right kind of people when you get a chance. I don't suppose you're going to vegetate in the country all your life, and you're old enough to take a little social interest in people if you're ever going to."

"Don't get on with them," said Garry, wringing the dish mop out with a vicious twist.

"You just don't want to, that's all."

Garry was thinking: "Don't for heaven's sake let's have this all over again!" for it was an old grievance of Kay's, though during the winter there had been little to bring the question up. Now, like the spring-time violets, it was rearing its head once more. Everyone couldn't be the same. Kay got along with one kind of person, she herself with another, and that was all there was to it.

There was a faintly noticeable change in Kay these days; she was a little bit on the defensive, a little bit— and rather suddenly—the grown-up sister. She was stricter with Caroline, more than usually fussy about the household generally. It was all a part of the change that had come over the whole hillside since the hammers first began to ring on the old house.

"Just as I knew it would be," Garry thought resentfully. "Everything comfortably settled and going along nicely, and then there's got to be an upheaval. I wish city people would stay in the city. Once we thought this place was quiet and look at it now—it's like an anthill!"

She worked off much of her discontent in the garden
—"eating worms," as Mary Rowe called that particular
frame of mind in which all the world seems out of
joint—finding a contrary pleasure in wearing her oldest
slacks and most disreputable sweaters, and taking comfort only in Emily, a consoling person whom one could
never imagine, under any circumstances, shaken or in-
fluenced by whatever went on around her. Kingdoms
might totter and skies fall, but Emily, thank heaven,
would always remain the same. Emily and Mary Rowe,
vastly different to the casual eye but alike in more ways
than one, which was perhaps why they got along so well
together.

It was during the week of warm weather—almost like
a bit of June tumbled out of place from the calendar—
that Martin created a diversion.

On Saturday morning he and Jimmie had set out early
for a walk, with sandwiches in their pockets. Emily
was enjoying one of her hard-working spells when the
typewriter clanked incessantly; Kay, after an early
lunch, had gone for a drive with Charles, and it was only
at four o'clock that Garry, busy outdoors, realized with
a start that neither of the boys had yet returned. She ran
across the road, where Shirley and Caroline were
playing.

READY FOR PENNY

"They're late," said Mary, "but they'll turn up. They were going to the Falls, back of the old Judd place, and they can't get lost anywhere round there. I'd worry if there was one alone, but there's two of them and they've both got sense. If they aren't back by the time Neal gets in I'll have him take the truck down along the road there and look for them."

Time went on, and still there were no boys. At five Garry began to get worried. She had gone back to look at the kitchen clock for the tenth time when Shirley and Caroline came flying across the road.

"Jimmie and Martin are back, and Martin got bit by a snake up at the Falls and he's got his leg all tied up and Jimmie says . . ."

For a second Garry's heart stood still. She saw Martin coming slowly up the path, a scared and white-faced Jimmie beside him, with Mary Rowe, almost as scared, at their heels. Martin's stocking was pulled down; he had a blood-stained handkerchief twisted round his leg and it seemed to Garry's horrified eyes that he swayed a little as he walked. Copperheads . . . was it Neal who had said once there were copperheads up at the Falls? Martin's body felt already limp as she got him into a chair. There was a horrible sick feeling deep inside her, but her voice managed to sound steady.

"What kind of snake was it, Martin? Did you see it?"

"Of course I saw it—I had it in my hands. I don't know what kind of snake it was. Anyway the darn thing bit me. Don't be scared, Garry. I've fixed the bite anyway."

"It was a spotted adder!" Jimmie insisted.

"It was not!"

"It was too!"

"Wasn't I holding it? I ought to know. Get me the snake book, Garry."

Little by little the story came out. The boys had reached the Falls and had gone in wading before they ate their lunch. Martin had found the snake on a rock ledge where it had crawled out into the sunshine, half torpid still from its winter sleep. It seemed dead, and he was playing with it when it suddenly came to in the warmth of his hand, twisted round and bit him unexpectedly on his bare leg. Up till then apparently he had been quite positive it was a harmless snake, but after that bite he wasn't so sure. Horrid doubts rose in his mind. He began to think maybe it wasn't such a harmless snake after all; its very markings looked different. But he knew what to do, and being Martin, he was thorough about it. He pulled out his pocketknife, set his teeth, and began to hack. The knife was blunt, and by the time he was through and the handkerchief tourniquet tightly and professionally twisted, his leg was beginning to throb in real earnest, and it throbbed more and more as he limped down the road, leaning on Jimmie's shoulder, to the farmhouse at the foot of the Falls, where they rested some time before the farmer drove them part way home in his car.

"But that must have been hours ago! Why didn't you telephone, do something! You mean you just sat there like two idiots, waiting for symptoms?"

"Well, I . . ."

"Well, we . . ."

There seemed a gap here in the story; just what had happened no one could make out. Garry's hands shook as she pulled the bandage off. There was a deep purple welt where the twisted linen had cut into Martin's leg and below it a nasty-looking mess of crisscross slashes.

"Shall I call the doctor?" Mary asked. "He has snake serum."

Caroline began to whimper, but Emily Humbold peered closely through her glasses.

"H-m. Did it hurt much when it first bit you?"

"It—no, it didn't. I don't remember. It just bit me."

"If it had been a poisonous snake you'd have felt it, all right; I know that much. Four hours ago. . . . I guess you'll be spared to us, Martin."

Garry insisted: "Martin, listen. Are you perfectly sure you'd know a copperhead if you saw one?"

"Of course 1 would!" Martin sounded irritable and unsteady. "I tell you it wasn't a copperhead; it was some other kind of snake. If you get me the darn snake book I'll find it. It wasn't till after it bit me that I thought maybe it looked kind of funny, and Jimmie got scared and the book says . . ."

Emily chuckled.

"That's right—when you do a job, do it thoroughly! Better get some hot water and iodine, Garry, and we'll wash this off."

Bathed and rebandaged, the wounded hero was left to rest on the sofa, poring over the snake book, while Caroline kept awed watch beside him. Emily went back to her typewriter. Garry, getting supper in the kitchen, turned an anxious eye from time to time towards the other room. In spite of Emily's words she was still uneasy. There was something queer about Martin; the way he acted, the way he looked. His eyes seemed unnatural, his face flushed. Supposing Emily was wrong—supposing snake poison could begin to work hours afterwards?

Caroline tiptoed in.

"Garry, I wish you'd come and look at Martin. He's breathing in an awful f-funny way!"

Garry crossed the floor in two strides. Martin certainly was breathing in a funny way. The snake book had slipped to the floor; he lay with his face half burrowed into the sofa pillow, and when Garry shook him, gently at first, then harder, he only gave a faint groan.

Coma . . . people did pass into a coma from snake venom. But it evidently wasn't coma in Martin's case. He sat up suddenly, stared at Garry with a greenish face, and thrusting her violently aside made a sudden dash for the back door.

It was at just that moment that Mary Rowe came hurrying over, opening the front door just as Martin disappeared at the back.

"Garry—what's the matter?"

"It's Martin. We've got to have the doctor! He's been looking awfully queer and dopey, and just this minute . . ."

Mary laughed.

"That's what I came over to tell you. Neal says don't worry about Martin. When he and Jimmie got to telling about that house where they stopped it set me thinking, and I just got the whole truth out of Jimmie this minute. They told the man there what had happened and I guess you know what the first aid for snake bite is, anywhere in the country—corn whiskey or applejack—and that man had no more sense than to fill Martin up with it instead of calling a doctor or letting us know. That's why they were so late coming back, only neither of them wanted to own up about it. I thought that story of just sitting in the house for three hours sounded fishy!"

Garry drew a breath. "So that's it! Mary, I was so scared!"

"Well, you don't have to be. Neal says there's never been a copperhead found anywhere near the Falls since he can remember, and what bit Martin must have been a milk snake; they will if you handle them roughly, especially in early spring when they're half torpid. I guess what really ailed him wasn't the snake, it was the cure!"

Martin recovered from both his remedies, self-inflicted and otherwise, with no worse reminder than a sore leg, and for several days no one was so inconsiderate as to mention snake bites in his presence. He and Jimmie were deep now in a new enterprise, the building of a cabin down by the little brook which ran through a corner of the Rowes' wood-lot, in which they could retreat from the world and live the simple life all alone. Neal told them they might have the lumber from an old shed which he had long intended to tear down, in return for the work of cleaning the site up tidily after them; Mary promised them the disused laundry stove in the wood-shed to cook over, and Garry a set of camp dishes, feeling that she owed Martin something for the lecture she had given him that evening in his bedroom after the snake episode. Building was in the air, and with a job of their own the boys were no longer hanging round the big house, interrupting the work and getting into mischief, a respite which Neal declared was cheap enough at the price of a bundle of shingles and a few pounds of nails.

The general fever had taken Shirley and Caroline, too. Left out of this venture they took possession of the disused corncrib which had long been a bone of contention. The sides had been boarded over, the roof was fairly water-tight, and the girls promised Caroline the leftovers of wall paper when the upstairs papering was through. That task was in full swing now, and Caroline followed every movement jealously, sighing as the rolls diminished one by one, and casting anguished looks at each slash of the scissors.

"We got two more rolls than it said to for your room, so there'll be plenty left over, and you needn't go pouncing on all those scraps and snippets as if they were so much gold! Here—you can have all these borders we aren't using, now, only for the love of heaven take it off somewhere and get out of the way!"

For with the lack of a stepladder Garry was perched uneasily on a soap box and a bedroom chair, which threatened at every moment to topple beneath her. Papering wasn't quite such a simple job as it had seemed at first; the paste stuck to everything but the walls, and the lengths of paper, smoothed down carefully as they were hung, broke out next instant in creases and blisters that no coaxing and patting would reduce.

"Don't worry. All that is supposed to come out afterwards as it dries," Kay remarked easily, looking on.

"I hope it does! This piece looks worse than chicken pox. I got the other side pretty even. Penny's room ought to be better. It's got a small pattern and it's easier to match."

Penny's room had been left till the last, so they could have more practice in the meantime. It was Garry who did most of the actual work; Kay was better at laying paint on than in wrestling with refractory objects like wall paper and paste brushes, and there was only one paste brush at that, so her share was chiefly in holding the lengths up, which she could do more easily, being the taller, while Garry smoothed and patted.

"It would be funny if after fixing this place all up we had to move right out of it," Garry said, eyeing the last bare strip of wall in Caroline's room.

"What do you mean?"

"Well, if they wanted the house back we'd have to. I was thinking of that this morning."

"I don't believe they will. Charles wouldn't be remodeling this house for another year or so. Maybe he won't even then; he likes what we've done to it so much that I guess it'll stay the way it is. Though it would be nice to have water piped down and a bathroom put in where the pantry is now, and if they're going to get electric light carried up the hill . . ."

Evidently Kay was changing her mind about the country considerably, in spite of what she might say about "vegetating." But perhaps that only applied to the winters. Garry gave her a quick look, but all she said was:

"No more frozen pumps! That would be a comfort, anyway."

Kay went downstairs to wash her hands and set the potatoes over for lunch; Garry pasted the last strip and hung it in place. The room looked nice with its gay rosebuds and little garlands. On the wall that was finished yesterday the paper lay smooth and taut, every telltale bubble vanished. She gave it a last critical look, set the windows wide open so the place could dry out, and went down to get in a precious half hour in the garden before midday.

One third of the vegetable patch behind the house was already dug up and raked, and Garry had planted two rows of early peas that should be up in another week. There was lettuce two inches high in the cold-frame and she was longing for the time to set out the cabbage and cauliflower seedlings already growing rank and leggy in their boxes. No one round here planted garden before May, Mary Rowe said, but Garry had her own ideas about starting things early. Meantime there was plenty to do, for weeds were coming up thick and fast in her pet cold-frame along with the lettuce and radishes, and the last few days had given her no time to attend to them.

It seemed she had barely settled down to work before Caroline came lagging round the corner of the house.

"I wanted to go down by the brook where the boys are, and Martin an' Jimmie are just awful mean and they started getting funny, and they say it's *their* place, an' Martin . . ."

"Well, they've only got Saturdays and after school to work in, and I guess they don't want you tagging round and hindering them," Garry returned, feeling a strong sympathy just then with the young house builders who wanted to make the most of their free moments. "Go ahead and start fixing your own place; there's plenty to do."

"We can't till we get the wall paper. You said you'd make us paste this afternoon, and I thought maybe——"

"Then think again! I'm not going to stop my work and make you paste right this minute, if that's what you're after. Can't I get *one* half hour quiet to myself?"

Caroline edged off before firing her parting shot.

"Well, anyway I just came round by the kitchen an'
the potatoes have started to burn, so I guess . . ."

Garry sat back violently on her heels.

"Oh, Lord! Where's Kay?"

"I saw her going up the road a while back. I did pull
the saucepan off, Garry, but I guess you better look at
them."

"I guess I had!"

Garry fled to the kitchen, where an only too-familiar
smell of burned saucepan greeted her nose; the kitchen
clock marked twelve-thirty. Creamed sauce still to make
for the mince, and the salad not even prepared.

"You think anyone wouldn't walk off up the road
without a word and leave potatoes to look after themselves all morning! What on earth's got into Kay anyway, these days?" she muttered as she clattered round.
"I'll attend to all this. You go wash your hands,
Caroline, and get the table set, *quick*. And then go up the
hill and tell Kay dinner's ready."

Everything was done, the cream sauce made, the rescued potatoes keeping hot in the oven, before Caroline
returned, alone and important.

"Where's Kay? Did you find her?"

"She said to go ahead and start. She an' Charles . . ."

"Mr. Bassett," Garry corrected.

[213]

"Well, you all call him Charles!"

"What grown-up people do doesn't include little girls. I suppose they were busy measuring or something."

"They weren't busy either," Caroline burst out. "If you want to know, they were just sittin' out on a rock back of the house, going chu-chu-chu about nothing at all with their heads together, and when I told Kay dinner was ready all she said was to run along and not come bothering."

Garry drew a long breath, staring at the minced ham.

"Heavens!" she thought to herself. "I wish Penny would hurry up and come back!"

Kay's Day

AS a matter of fact there had been something rather odd
about Penny's letters lately. Usually she wrote long and
gossipy accounts of everything, the people she met, all
the little things that she and Peggy had been doing. But
her last few letters had seemed unaccountably flat; tame
notes referring to this and that but giving no particular
news, except that everything was all right and she hoped
to be home before long. If not exactly constrained they
were so unlike her natural self that Kay grew quite
concerned.

"Isn't she funny? She doesn't mention a single thing
that was in our last letters, and she must have had them
by now. I just don't make it out. She might tell us a little
more."

"Maybe she's just fed up with the place and can't
think of anything new to write about," Garry suggested.

Kay frowned. "The whole thing is so sort of detached
and funny, but the writing looks all right. She couldn't

be having a nervous breakdown or something, and Peggy not wanting to tell us?"

"Not Penny. I tell you, Kay, she's been writing long letters all winter and now she's suddenly got bored with it. That's what it reads like to me. It's the sort of stuff you write when you have to fill a page in and don't know what to say. I've done it myself."

But that explanation didn't satisfy Kay, haunted by visions of a changed and preoccupied Penny, too busy with her own thoughts and affairs to be interested in other people's. Nothing about their own eagerness to have her home again, but just pleasant little references to the weather and sitting in the sun. If that was what a winter in New Mexico did to one . . .

Meantime she stitched away at the curtains she was making for Penny's room, pale green glazed chintz with a piping of dull rose to go with the new wall paper. Martin had given up the best part of one precious holiday to scraping and waxing the old painted bureau that had always looked so shabby, while Caroline hung about disconsolately until Garry had a bright idea.

"I tell you what. You make her a dish garden. You can use that flat blue bowl on the top pantry shelf. Fix it with moss and Quaker ladies and it'll look lovely on her window ledge."

"But they'll die before Penny gets here," objected

Caroline, who had been counting the days off one by one
on the grocery calendar in the kitchen, seeing in her
mind's eye the long space yet to cover before the little
black crosses reached to the end of the month.

"If they do you can always get fresh ones. Don't be
such a misery, but go and start it right now. Take a basket
and you can have my trowel to dig them up with; it's out
there by the cold-frame."

The arranging and rearranging of that dish garden
took most of Caroline's attention for days to come. She
planted it over at least a dozen times, and whenever she
was needed to set the table or dry the silver it always
happened that she was busy "fixing Penny's garden,"
but at least it gave her something to think about during
the days of waiting. For there was still no news of the
exact date of Penny's arrival, and still those brief pleasant letters arrived at intervals of a few days each, regular as clockwork.

"Suppose she never did come home," said Garry one
morning. "Suppose we just keep getting these queer letters day by day, and nothing else ever happens.
Suppose . . ."

But at this gruesome suggestion Caroline began to
snivel, and Kay said sharply: "Don't tease the child like
that! You're getting her all worked up."

"I was only fooling. Don't be silly, Caroline."

[217]

"Well, when you're fooling you sound like you weren't fooling, and I don't like it!"

"Ambrose Bierce just disappeared and nobody ever found him," said Martin, who kept curious and unexpected bits of information stored in his mind, to produce usually at inopportune moments. "And Neal said there was a man once lived over on Seven Hill and one day he just walked out of his front door and nobody ever saw him again."

"Which is exactly," said Garry, "what I would like to do myself, one of these days."

She wandered out into the spring sunshine where Emily was playing ball with Arabella. Hands clasped round her knees, she sat watching the tiny racing figure, so like a skein of orange wool blown to and fro by the wind, until Emily said abruptly: "That'll do," put the ball in her pocket and turned, while Arabella dropped panting on the grass.

"What's the trouble?"

"Spring," said Garry, digging her fingers viciously into the soft earth beside her. "Doesn't it ever get you that way? I'm cross and disagreeable and restless. I want to do something and I don't know what I want to do. I'd like to walk out on everything and go some place where I'd never been before—and *stay* there!"

"Heavens!" said Emily, looking at her with interest.

"I mean it."

"I'm sure you do. Everyone gets like that once in a while. Usually it's the result of too much family. I know all the symptoms. It gets you all of a sudden, like measles." She spoke jokingly but her sharp eyes lingered on Garry's face, for she had been well aware of those symptoms for some time. It had been a long winter, and most of its responsibilities had fallen on Garry's shoulders, sturdy, but not sturdy enough to go on forever without rebellion. "Did you ever sit down and think," she went on cheerfully, "just what you would do if you suddenly came into a fortune? Not a big fortune, but a nice comfortable-sized one, that you could do what you liked with."

"I know exactly what I'd do," said Garry, falling promptly into the game. "I'd send Kay to Europe for two years, first of all. I'd have Martin prepared for college. Then I'd see that Penny and Caroline were settled somewhere comfortably—or they could go on a trip if they wanted to."

"In fact, everyone nicely placed." Emily nodded, thoroughly enjoying this little insight. "You make me think of a hen with a bunch of chickens. And then what?"

Garry grinned suddenly.

"Then I'd take what money I might need for emergencies myself, and put it in a bank some place. And I'd

start out and work my way all around the country, taking
different jobs just as they happened and trying any darn
thing I fancied that would support me for as long as I
was interested in it. It may sound crazy," she went on,
ruffling Arabella's orange mane as she spoke, "but I've
often wondered whether a person couldn't do that if they
really set their mind to it, and I'd like to try it out. Maybe
I'd get clear across the continent and maybe I wouldn't
get any further than the next township, but I'd have a
swell time trying."

"What kind of jobs?"

"Anything. I don't mean swanky jobs. Any old thing
that would pay my way as I went along. There's nearly
always something that somebody wants done, if you look
around you."

"True," said Emily.

"I'd like to know what it feels like to wait on table or
work in a store or pick fruit, or . . . oh, just the sort of
things anyone could do."

"You might advertise," said Emily meanly.

"If I did," Garry retorted, "I bet I'd write an ad that
would get me the kind I want, anyway. Hello, there's
the mailman."

She jumped up and strolled down to the gateway
where the dusty creaking car had just come to a pause on
its way downhill. A queer sort of castle in the air, Emily

Humbold thought, watching the straight swing of her shoulders, but there was one thing about Garry; she never wove schemes about things that she couldn't do.

"All for you, as usual. There's a card about some auction; we'll keep that for Penny. Oh, and a letter for Kay."

Kay was indoors, turning the last hem on Penny's curtains. She looked at the envelope heading.

"Another refusal. Well, they've taken a little longer about it, this time."

"Open it and see. Heavens, Kay, don't be such a poke! What did I tell you?"

For Kay's face had changed as she read the closely typewritten page.

"They like it. It's some woman writing and she wants me to come there and talk it over with her. She doesn't say for certain, but it sounds as if they were interested." The color had rushed into Kay's cheeks. "Look, Garry, do you suppose that really does mean anything?"

"Of course it does. Do you imagine she'd drag you all the way up to town to talk it over if it didn't."

"She only says 'if I'm likely to be in town any time soon.' "

"You're likely to be in town tomorrow morning. You'll make that eight-o'clock train if I have to push you on it." Garry had taken prompt command of the situation. "You'll have time to see these people and settle everything, and get the afternoon train back again. Edna will take you down."

There was no need for Edna or the train journey either, for as soon as Charles heard the news he offered to drive Kay into the city and back. He had business in town himself that could just as well be done tomorrow as any other day. It was to be an early start, with breakfast along the road, and as Kay swallowed a hasty cup of coffee next morning she gave a last anxious look at the plain tailored suit, carefully pressed the night before from its winter creases, the town shoes that Garry had finally located after long search in one of the attic trunks, and Cousin Carrie's Christmas silk stockings, useful now for the first time.

"Do I look all right?"

"Fine. Stop at the first decent store you come to and buy gloves, and you can leave that old pair in the car. And remember—act big and don't let them talk you down. And don't you sign any contract till Emily has looked it over for you. Good-bye and good luck!"

Garry waved vigorously as the roadster sped down the hill, feeling that she had done her best, anyway, towards launching Kay on the high road to success.

With the children off to school ten minutes earlier than usual there was a long and tranquil day ahead.

KAY'S DAY

Garry basked in the feeling of freedom and leisure that comes over any member of a family, no matter how united, when all the other members are comfortably off and out of the way. She tidied the house, baked a chocolate cake for supper, feeling unusually energetic, and set it to cool while she wandered over to the Rowes', to find Mary busy over her washtub in the kitchen while Tommy amused himself with a saucepan, a strainer, and a pail of soapsuds, making soup with the gravel outside the back door. It was long since she had had a good gossip with Mary, and the time flew until Neal's overalled figure, suddenly blocking the doorway, reminded her of lunch and a hungry Emily waiting across the road.

"Half the day gone," Garry thought guiltily. "And I was going to get Penny's curtains up and the rest of the garden dug."

"I expect I'll have to be packing my things before so very long," Emily remarked casually as they sat over their coffee in the living room.

"You?" Garry stared at her in sudden dismay. "Indeed you won't. Why, you're one of the family. Penny would be furious if you were gone before she got here, after all we've written about you. We want you to stay all summer. Unless you don't like it any more," she added. "Maybe you've got something else to do."

"I'd rather stay, if it's all right really. For a while

anyway. Charles has a room planned for me up at his house, when he ever gets it done. But I like it better here. There'll be so many comings and goings up at that place and I'm like Arabella—I enjoy quiet. Besides, I'm an incorrigibly untidy person, as you know, and by the time they get the house up there all planned and perfect there won't be any place in it for untidiness."

Their eyes met and they both smiled, sharing the same ideas about comfort as opposed to perfection.

"Isn't it funny how things turn out!" Garry looked through the window and up the hill to where the new shingles caught the sunlight. "When we first came to live here we used to wonder about that house, and Kay was always saying how she'd love to have a hand in the fixing over of it. Ever since I can remember we've always joked about 'Kay's ideas' and teased her about wanting everything just so. With us I guess it's been mostly a case of plenty to fix and nothing to fix it with, but now she's really got a chance to show what she can do for once."

Penny's curtains could wait till tomorrow, she decided as she stacked the lunch dishes. Kay still had to sew the rings on, and Penny couldn't possibly be home for another week, since they had had another of those queer noncommittal letters only the day before yesterday. The garden was another matter; it was too good a day to spend indoors, and when the kitchen was tidy she took spade and rake and set to work.

It was a pleasant drowsy afternoon. Robins were busy round the apple trees where pale sticky buds were already unfolding, and the click of Emily's typewriter sounded lazily through the open window. Arabella wandered out presently, picking her ladylike way over the fresh-turned earth, with one eye on the coon cat who sat erect and motionless among the pasture weeds, watching a mole-run. Kay wouldn't be back till five at the earliest, but Garry was so impatient to know the result of that journey that she found herself listening every moment for the possible hum of a car down the valley. But the children came back from school, supper was over and cleared away, before at last the roadster drew up at the gate.

It needed only one look at Kay's face to know the news.

"It's all settled—they're going to use it. Oh Garry, you don't know how I feel! Hey, look out!"

For Garry had seized her in a sudden whirl that nearly landed them both on the floor.

"Never mind. I've squashed your hat, but you can buy a new one now. What happened? Sit down and tell me all about it."

"It'll be published this fall. There's some work I've

got to do on it still; one picture to draw over again, and the end papers. I never thought about those. But that won't take very long. I must have stayed there two hours and she was perfectly grand; showed me some of the other books they are making, and just how things are printed, and the sort of colors one can use—ever so many things I'd never known about and always wanted to. I never knew there was so much went to making just one book! And the best of it is, it's got me started on new ideas now, and I can't wait to begin on them."

"It's the feeling of having really made a beginning that counts so much," she said later that evening, after Charles had gone, the last remnants of the chocolate cake were finished, and she and Garry were sitting curled on the sofa watching the flames in the open fireplace—for evenings were still chilly. "When I saw all those other things there today my own stuff began to look pretty awful. I just hated to look at it, spread out there. I could see all the mistakes I'd made and all that I might have put into it and hadn't. But I guess everyone feels that way when you come to measure up, the first time. I haven't got any illusions about it, either. But it did make me feel that the next thing I try I'll be able to do a lot better, and if they do like my stuff at all I'm going to try hard, and I'll turn out something very different. Garry, I'm so glad you made me stick at those drawings, even if they did seem silly. It's just groping along by oneself that's so awful; I got into a kind of muddle this winter when it didn't seem as if anything was worth trying. Charles gave me a good talking to coming back in the car today. We nearly quarreled over it, but I guess he was right."

Garry looked sharply up; there was a little flush on Kay's cheeks, but she went on quickly: "Oh, I know what's back of your mind, but you don't have to worry. We're just good friends and he's got work to think about and so have I, but he's the first person I've ever met that I can really talk to about things, and who understands."

"That's how it always begins," thought Garry, giving a poke to the smoldering logs.

"I don't mean that you don't. I only mean . . ."

"I know just what you mean," said Garry, sitting back on her heels. "You mean someone outside the family, someone who hasn't watched you grow up and who doesn't think they know all about you. That's exactly why I like Emily and Mary Rowe. When I want to spill things over I can spill it over to them, and it's all right. They don't get their feelings hurt and they don't immediately think that anything you happen to say has some relation to something or other they happened to say or do ten months back. I know!"

"Well, that's how I do feel. And that's why . . ."

A prolonged and dismal hoot broke suddenly on the stillness.

"Listen!" said Garry. She dropped the poker and moved to the open window. "Sounds like some car in trouble down the hill there."

Kay joined her. They stood looking out down the road to where on the first twisting rise two headlights blinked uncertainly, while the grating whine of gears sounded, stopped, and began again.

"Stalled on the first turn. Someone who doesn't know the road, or they're out of gas."

"Maybe it's Neal," Kay said.

"Neal's back ages ago. It's after eleven now. Besides, that doesn't sound like his car."

"Well, we don't have to help them out. Garry, I'm going to bed. That drive made me so sleepy!"

But Garry still stood there, peering out. The car had started anew, hung for a moment doubtfully, then lurched forward, taking the zigzag climb with much wobbling and groaning but a dogged determination that brought it at last, with a final burst of power, just abreast of their own gateway, where it stalled again for good. A slim figure got out, and with one amazed look Garry tore the front door open and ran down the path.

"Penny!"

"It's me. I never thought I'd make it. I've had that

wretched hill on my mind ever since I started out. Did I wake the whole countryside up?"

"But Penny—Kay, come here!" Garry shook the small figure to make sure it was real. "You mean you learned to drive and you drove all that way alone!"

"Every inch of it." Penny waved her hand at the shabby flivver, dust-colored, with dried mud caked to the axles, and one crumpled fender visible in the dim glow from the headlights. "We bought that wreck down there for forty dollars and Peggy said if I wanted to drive it back I could keep it, and there it is. I'd planned to creep up and take you all by surprise, seeing it was after dark, and then I had to stall on the hill! The horn was an accident; I leaned on the button. Well, I've stalled my way half across the country, come to that, but I got here!"

They hugged, held each other at arm's length to stare, and hugged again.

"You're looking grand!"

She was. A grimy and disheveled Penny when they dragged her indoors to the lamplight, almost as dust-smeared as the car, but amazingly sun tanned, firm of muscle under her khaki flannel shirt and with a new light of assurance in her eyes.

"Where are the rest of you?"

But Martin had already stumbled out of bed, roused

by the sound of the car, Caroline came trailing down in her nightgown, only half awake; Emily Humbold loomed in her doorway, stalwart in striped pyjamas, clutching an outraged Arabella who had no opinion at all of midnight strangers falling from the skies like this. A state of happy confusion in which everyone talked at once and nobody listened and news went in at one ear and out at the other, since nothing seemed particularly important except the great fact that Penny was home again, until suddenly she said:

"Father's coming back in June, for a few weeks. I didn't write about it because he didn't want me to tell you until he was quite sure. He'll be busy most of the time but he'll be able to get up here for a little while anyway."

"He is? Oh, grand! And Kay's sold a book. What do you think of that?"

"You're not fooling? Kay, let me look at you! Tell me about it."

"I'll tell you tomorrow. There's too much else to think about now. Penny, we have missed you so!"

"If you ask me you've done remarkably well without me!" Penny looked happily round on the familiar room in which her mind had lived for so much of the time that she was away.

"But Penny, those letters!" Garry suddenly remembered. "How on earth . . ."

The old guilty expression came over their mother's face, what they always used to call "Penny's auction look."

"Well, you see . . . I didn't want to tell you what I was doing because I knew you'd be worried. So I wrote all those letters ahead and gave them to Margaret—I told you she is down there with Peggy now?—and I numbered them all and told her to mail one every four days. And I had her forward yours to me along the road so I'd know *you* were all right."

"Worried! Do you know you had us crazy?" demanded Garry. "We thought you were having a nervous breakdown or something, from those letters, and didn't want to tell us. They were so absolutely unlike you. Some day I'm going to make you read them over, every one, and you'll see!"

"Well, it's awfully hard to make up letters ahead of time that way, but I did think I'd done them pretty well. And then I got to the point where I simply had to write you postcards, but I didn't dare mail them so I had to put them by, and today I dumped the whole lot in the mailbox in some little New York town I came through. You'll get them tomorrow, all in one bunch.

When that postmaster sorts the mail I guess he'll think someone was crazy."

"He wouldn't be far wrong, either. Now we know where the strain comes from in this family!"

"Sheer guilty conscience," Penny confessed. "I felt so selfish, having a perfectly good time all by myself without you knowing. It was the first time in years I've ever done exactly as I pleased, with no one to consider. I could stop when I chose and go on when I chose. I slept in any odd tourist camp I took a fancy to. I didn't have to stop and eat unless I felt like it and I didn't have to talk to a single soul unless I chose. I had a perfectly marvelous time."

Garry nodded. She, more than anyone else, knew exactly how Penny had felt. This growing-up business —perhaps it didn't after all make so much difference as one thought. Or did anyone really grow up at all?

"Well, I guess we'll forgive you. Only next time . . ."

"There won't be a next time," Penny sighed happily. "I'm going to stay put, now."

"We were going to have everything fixed up to welcome you, and here we're still at sixes and sevens and your curtains aren't hung and your bed isn't made and all that's ready is Caroline's dish garden," Kay laughed. "If she hasn't just un-fixed it all over again!"

"I didn't. It's right here. I'm going to get fresh violets tomorrow."

Caroline looked with self-satisfaction at the little bowl of moss and flowers on the table at Penny's elbow, over which she had labored so persistently.

"Do we have to go to school tomorrow?" Martin asked.

"No, you don't, but you have to go to bed tonight." Penny jumped up. "Do you realize it's tomorrow now, and I haven't even got my suitcase out of the car!"

"I'll fetch the flashlight."

They stood in the doorway looking out over the quiet hillside. The night air was damp and mild, filled with the smell of earth and of springtime; from down in the valley came the glad minor chorus of the peepers in the swamp. Across the road the lantern in the Rowes' kitchen gleamed faintly through the tangled apple boughs. There was a light in an upper room too, that only Kay's eyes saw and rested on, before she turned to slip her arm round Penny's waist with a little sigh of contentment.

"It's good to have you back!"

"It's good to be back."

Garry stretched her arms, waiting for Martin to bring the suitcase. It was more than a gesture; she had a feeling as though something had slipped from her shoulders. It was a little like the feeling she had had that night

[233]

WINTERBOUND

when she woke up in the darkness and knew all at
once that the cold snap had broken; a sense of something
different in the air, a feeling of security and comfort,
that everything, now, was going to be all right.

A CATALOG OF SELECTED DOVER
BOOKS IN ALL FIELDS OF INTEREST

100 BEST-LOVED POEMS, Edited by Philip Smith. "The Passionate Shepherd to His Love," "Shall I compare thee to a summer's day?" "Death, be not proud," "The Raven," "The Road Not Taken," plus works by Blake, Wordsworth, Byron, Shelley, Keats, many others. 96pp. 5³⁄₁₆ x 8¼.   0-486-28553-7

100 SMALL HOUSES OF THE THIRTIES, Brown-Blodgett Company. Exterior photographs and floor plans for 100 charming structures. Illustrations of models accompanied by descriptions of interiors, color schemes, closet space, and other amenities. 200 illustrations. 112pp. 8⅜ x 11.   0-486-44131-8

1000 TURN-OF-THE-CENTURY HOUSES: With Illustrations and Floor Plans, Herbert C. Chivers. Reproduced from a rare edition, this showcase of homes ranges from cottages and bungalows to sprawling mansions. Each house is meticulously illustrated and accompanied by complete floor plans. 256pp. 9⅜ x 12¼.

    0-486-45596-3

101 GREAT AMERICAN POEMS, Edited by The American Poetry & Literacy Project. Rich treasury of verse from the 19th and 20th centuries includes works by Edgar Allan Poe, Robert Frost, Walt Whitman, Langston Hughes, Emily Dickinson, T. S. Eliot, other notables. 96pp. 5³⁄₁₆ x 8¼.   0-486-40158-8

101 GREAT SAMURAI PRINTS, Utagawa Kuniyoshi. Kuniyoshi was a master of the warrior woodblock print — and these 18th-century illustrations represent the pinnacle of his craft. Full-color portraits of renowned Japanese samurais pulse with movement, passion, and remarkably fine detail. 112pp. 8⅜ x 11.   0-486-46523-3

ABC OF BALLET, Janet Grosser. Clearly worded, abundantly illustrated little guide defines basic ballet-related terms: arabesque, battement, pas de chat, relevé, sissonne, many others. Pronunciation guide included. Excellent primer. 48pp. 4³⁄₁₆ x 5¾.

    0-486-40871-X

ACCESSORIES OF DRESS: An Illustrated Encyclopedia, Katherine Lester and Bess Viola Oerke. Illustrations of hats, veils, wigs, cravats, shawls, shoes, gloves, and other accessories enhance an engaging commentary that reveals the humor and charm of the many-sided story of accessorized apparel. 644 figures and 59 plates. 608pp. 6⅛ x 9¼.

    0-486-43378-1

ADVENTURES OF HUCKLEBERRY FINN, Mark Twain. Join Huck and Jim as their boyhood adventures along the Mississippi River lead them into a world of excitement, danger, and self-discovery. Humorous narrative, lyrical descriptions of the Mississippi valley, and memorable characters. 224pp. 5³⁄₁₆ x 8¼.   0-486-28061-6

ALICE STARMORE'S BOOK OF FAIR ISLE KNITTING, Alice Starmore. A noted designer from the region of Scotland's Fair Isle explores the history and techniques of this distinctive, stranded-color knitting style and provides copious illustrated instructions for 14 original knitwear designs. 208pp. 8⅜ x 10⅞.   0-486-47218-3

ALICE'S ADVENTURES IN WONDERLAND, Lewis Carroll. Beloved classic about a little girl lost in a topsy-turvy land and her encounters with the White Rabbit, March Hare, Mad Hatter, Cheshire Cat, and other delightfully improbable characters. 42 illustrations by Sir John Tenniel. 96pp. 5³⁄₁₆ x 8¼.   0-486-27543-4

AMERICA'S LIGHTHOUSES: An Illustrated History, Francis Ross Holland. Profusely illustrated fact-filled survey of American lighthouses since 1716. Over 200 stations — East, Gulf, and West coasts, Great Lakes, Hawaii, Alaska, Puerto Rico, the Virgin Islands, and the Mississippi and St. Lawrence Rivers. 240pp. 8 x 10¾.
0-486-25576-X

AN ENCYCLOPEDIA OF THE VIOLIN, Alberto Bachmann. Translated by Frederick H. Martens. Introduction by Eugene Ysaye. First published in 1925, this renowned reference remains unsurpassed as a source of essential information, from construction and evolution to repertoire and technique. Includes a glossary and 73 illustrations. 496pp. 6⅛ x 9¼.   0-486-46618-3

ANIMALS: 1,419 Copyright-Free Illustrations of Mammals, Birds, Fish, Insects, etc., Selected by Jim Harter. Selected for its visual impact and ease of use, this outstanding collection presents over 1,000 species of animals in extremely lifelike poses. Includes mammals, birds, reptiles, amphibians, fish, insects, and other invertebrates. 284pp. 9 x 12.   0-486-23766-4

THE ANNALS, Tacitus. Translated by Alfred John Church and William Jackson Brodribb. This vital chronicle of Imperial Rome, written by the era's great historian, spans A.D. 14-68 and paints incisive psychological portraits of major figures, from Tiberius to Nero. 416pp. 5³⁄₁₆ x 8¼.   0-486-45236-0

ANTIGONE, Sophocles. Filled with passionate speeches and sensitive probing of moral and philosophical issues, this powerful and often-performed Greek drama reveals the grim fate that befalls the children of Oedipus. Footnotes. 64pp. 5³⁄₁₆ x 8 ¼.   0-486-27804-2

ART DECO DECORATIVE PATTERNS IN FULL COLOR, Christian Stoll. Reprinted from a rare 1910 portfolio, 160 sensuous and exotic images depict a breathtaking array of florals, geometrics, and abstracts — all elegant in their stark simplicity. 64pp. 8⅜ x 11.   0-486-44862-2

THE ARTHUR RACKHAM TREASURY: 86 Full-Color Illustrations, Arthur Rackham. Selected and Edited by Jeff A. Menges. A stunning treasury of 86 full-page plates span the famed English artist's career, from *Rip Van Winkle* (1905) to masterworks such as *Undine, A Midsummer Night's Dream,* and *Wind in the Willows* (1939). 96pp. 8⅜ x 11.
0-486-44685-9

THE AUTHENTIC GILBERT & SULLIVAN SONGBOOK, W. S. Gilbert and A. S. Sullivan. The most comprehensive collection available, this songbook includes selections from every one of Gilbert and Sullivan's light operas. Ninety-two numbers are presented uncut and unedited, and in their original keys. 410pp. 9 x 12.
0-486-23482-7

THE AWAKENING, Kate Chopin. First published in 1899, this controversial novel of a New Orleans wife's search for love outside a stifling marriage shocked readers. Today, it remains a first-rate narrative with superb characterization. New introductory Note. 128pp. 5³⁄₁₆ x 8¼.   0-486-27786-0

BASIC DRAWING, Louis Priscilla. Beginning with perspective, this commonsense manual progresses to the figure in movement, light and shade, anatomy, drapery, composition, trees and landscape, and outdoor sketching. Black-and-white illustrations throughout. 128pp. 8⅜ x 11.   0-486-45815-6

THE BATTLES THAT CHANGED HISTORY, Fletcher Pratt. Historian profiles 16 crucial conflicts, ancient to modern, that changed the course of Western civilization. Gripping accounts of battles led by Alexander the Great, Joan of Arc, Ulysses S. Grant, other commanders. 27 maps. 352pp. 5⅜ x 8½.   0-486-41129-X

BEETHOVEN'S LETTERS, Ludwig van Beethoven. Edited by Dr. A. C. Kalischer. Features 457 letters to fellow musicians, friends, greats, patrons, and literary men. Reveals musical thoughts, quirks of personality, insights, and daily events. Includes 15 plates. 410pp. 5⅜ x 8½.   0-486-22769-3

BERNICE BOBS HER HAIR AND OTHER STORIES, F. Scott Fitzgerald. This brilliant anthology includes 6 of Fitzgerald's most popular stories: "The Diamond as Big as the Ritz," the title tale, "The Offshore Pirate," "The Ice Palace," "The Jelly Bean," and "May Day." 176pp. 5⅜ x 8½.   0-486-47049-0

BESLER'S BOOK OF FLOWERS AND PLANTS: 73 Full-Color Plates from Hortus Eystettensis, 1613, Basilius Besler. Here is a selection of magnificent plates from the *Hortus Eystettensis*, which vividly illustrated and identified the plants, flowers, and trees that thrived in the legendary German garden at Eichstätt. 80pp. 8⅜ x 11.   0-486-46005-3

THE BOOK OF KELLS, Edited by Blanche Cirker. Painstakingly reproduced from a rare facsimile edition, this volume contains full-page decorations, portraits, illustrations, plus a sampling of textual leaves with exquisite calligraphy and ornamentation. 32 full-color illustrations. 32pp. 9⅜ x 12¼.   0-486-24345-1

THE BOOK OF THE CROSSBOW: With an Additional Section on Catapults and Other Siege Engines, Ralph Payne-Gallwey. Fascinating study traces history and use of crossbow as military and sporting weapon, from Middle Ages to modern times. Also covers related weapons: balistas, catapults, Turkish bows, more. Over 240 illustrations. 400pp. 7¼ x 10⅝.   0-486-28720-3

THE BUNGALOW BOOK: Floor Plans and Photos of 112 Houses, 1910, Henry L. Wilson. Here are 112 of the most popular and economic blueprints of the early 20th century — plus an illustration or photograph of each completed house. A wonderful time capsule that still offers a wealth of valuable insights. 160pp. 8⅜ x 11.   0-486-45104-6

THE CALL OF THE WILD, Jack London. A classic novel of adventure, drawn from London's own experiences as a Klondike adventurer, relating the story of a heroic dog caught in the brutal life of the Alaska Gold Rush. Note. 64pp. 5³⁄₁₆ x 8¼.   0-486-26472-6

CANDIDE, Voltaire. Edited by Francois-Marie Arouet. One of the world's great satires since its first publication in 1759. Witty, caustic skewering of romance, science, philosophy, religion, government — nearly all human ideals and institutions. 112pp. 5³⁄₁₆ x 8¼.   0-486-26689-3

CELEBRATED IN THEIR TIME: Photographic Portraits from the George Grantham Bain Collection, Edited by Amy Pastan. With an Introduction by Michael Carlebach. Remarkable portrait gallery features 112 rare images of Albert Einstein, Charlie Chaplin, the Wright Brothers, Henry Ford, and other luminaries from the worlds of politics, art, entertainment, and industry. 128pp. 8⅜ x 11.   0-486-46754-6

CHARIOTS FOR APOLLO: The NASA History of Manned Lunar Spacecraft to 1969, Courtney G. Brooks, James M. Grimwood, and Loyd S. Swenson, Jr. This illustrated history by a trio of experts is the definitive reference on the Apollo spacecraft and lunar modules. It traces the vehicles' design, development, and operation in space. More than 100 photographs and illustrations. 576pp. 6¾ x 9¼. 0-486-46756-2

Browse over 9,000 books at www.doverpublications.com

A CHRISTMAS CAROL, Charles Dickens. This engrossing tale relates Ebenezer Scrooge's ghostly journeys through Christmases past, present, and future and his ultimate transformation from a harsh and grasping old miser to a charitable and compassionate human being. 80pp. 5³⁄₁₆ x 8¼. 0-486-26865-9

COMMON SENSE, Thomas Paine. First published in January of 1776, this highly influential landmark document clearly and persuasively argued for American separation from Great Britain and paved the way for the Declaration of Independence. 64pp. 5³⁄₁₆ x 8¼. 0-486-29602-4

THE COMPLETE SHORT STORIES OF OSCAR WILDE, Oscar Wilde. Complete texts of "The Happy Prince and Other Tales," "A House of Pomegranates," "Lord Arthur Savile's Crime and Other Stories," "Poems in Prose," and "The Portrait of Mr. W. H." 208pp. 5³⁄₁₆ x 8¼. 0-486-45216-6

COMPLETE SONNETS, William Shakespeare. Over 150 exquisite poems deal with love, friendship, the tyranny of time, beauty's evanescence, death, and other themes in language of remarkable power, precision, and beauty. Glossary of archaic terms. 80pp. 5³⁄₁₆ x 8¼. 0-486-26686-9

THE COUNT OF MONTE CRISTO: Abridged Edition, Alexandre Dumas. Falsely accused of treason, Edmond Dantès is imprisoned in the bleak Chateau d'If. After a hair-raising escape, he launches an elaborate plot to extract a bitter revenge against those who betrayed him. 448pp. 5³⁄₁₆ x 8¼. 0-486-45643-9

CRAFTSMAN BUNGALOWS: Designs from the Pacific Northwest, Yoho & Merritt. This reprint of a rare catalog, showcasing the charming simplicity and cozy style of Craftsman bungalows, is filled with photos of completed homes, plus floor plans and estimated costs. An indispensable resource for architects, historians, and illustrators. 112pp. 10 x 7. 0-486-46875-5

CRAFTSMAN BUNGALOWS: 59 Homes from "The Craftsman," Edited by Gustav Stickley. Best and most attractive designs from Arts and Crafts Movement publication — 1903–1916 — includes sketches, photographs of homes, floor plans, descriptive text. 128pp. 8¼ x 11. 0-486-25829-7

CRIME AND PUNISHMENT, Fyodor Dostoyevsky. Translated by Constance Garnett. Supreme masterpiece tells the story of Raskolnikov, a student tormented by his own thoughts after he murders an old woman. Overwhelmed by guilt and terror, he confesses and goes to prison. 480pp. 5³⁄₁₆ x 8¼. 0-486-41587-2

THE DECLARATION OF INDEPENDENCE AND OTHER GREAT DOCUMENTS OF AMERICAN HISTORY: 1775-1865, Edited by John Grafton. Thirteen compelling and influential documents: Henry's "Give Me Liberty or Give Me Death," Declaration of Independence, The Constitution, Washington's First Inaugural Address, The Monroe Doctrine, The Emancipation Proclamation, Gettysburg Address, more. 64pp. 5³⁄₁₆ x 8¼. 0-486-41124-9

THE DESERT AND THE SOWN: Travels in Palestine and Syria, Gertrude Bell. "The female Lawrence of Arabia," Gertrude Bell wrote captivating, perceptive accounts of her travels in the Middle East. This intriguing narrative, accompanied by 160 photos, traces her 1905 sojourn in Lebanon, Syria, and Palestine. 368pp. 5⅜ x 8½.
0-486-46876-3

A DOLL'S HOUSE, Henrik Ibsen. Ibsen's best-known play displays his genius for realistic prose drama. An expression of women's rights, the play climaxes when the central character, Nora, rejects a smothering marriage and life in "a doll's house." 80pp. 5³⁄₁₆ x 8¼. 0-486-27062-9

DOOMED SHIPS: Great Ocean Liner Disasters, William H. Miller, Jr. Nearly 200 photographs, many from private collections, highlight tales of some of the vessels whose pleasure cruises ended in catastrophe: the *Morro Castle, Normandie, Andrea Doria, Europa,* and many others. 128pp. 8⅜ x 11¾. 0-486-45366-9

THE DORÉ BIBLE ILLUSTRATIONS, Gustave Doré. Detailed plates from the Bible: the Creation scenes, Adam and Eve, horrifying visions of the Flood, the battle sequences with their monumental crowds, depictions of the life of Jesus, 241 plates in all. 241pp. 9 x 12. 0-486-23004-X

DRAWING DRAPERY FROM HEAD TO TOE, Cliff Young. Expert guidance on how to draw shirts, pants, skirts, gloves, hats, and coats on the human figure, including folds in relation to the body, pull and crush, action folds, creases, more. Over 200 drawings. 48pp. 8¼ x 11. 0-486-45591-2

DUBLINERS, James Joyce. A fine and accessible introduction to the work of one of the 20th century's most influential writers, this collection features 15 tales, including a masterpiece of the short-story genre, "The Dead." 160pp. 5³⁄₁₆ x 8¼. 0-486-26870-5

EASY-TO-MAKE POP-UPS, Joan Irvine. Illustrated by Barbara Reid. Dozens of wonderful ideas for three-dimensional paper fun — from holiday greeting cards with moving parts to a pop-up menagerie. Easy-to-follow, illustrated instructions for more than 30 projects. 299 black-and-white illustrations. 96pp. 8⅜ x 11. 0-486-44622-0

EASY-TO-MAKE STORYBOOK DOLLS: A "Novel" Approach to Cloth Dollmaking, Sherralyn St. Clair. Favorite fictional characters come alive in this unique beginner's dollmaking guide. Includes patterns for Pollyanna, Dorothy from *The Wonderful Wizard of Oz,* Mary of *The Secret Garden,* plus easy-to-follow instructions, 263 black-and-white illustrations, and an 8-page color insert. 112pp. 8¼ x 11. 0-486-47360-0

EINSTEIN'S ESSAYS IN SCIENCE, Albert Einstein. Speeches and essays in accessible, everyday language profile influential physicists such as Niels Bohr and Isaac Newton. They also explore areas of physics to which the author made major contributions. 128pp. 5 x 8. 0-486-47011-3

EL DORADO: Further Adventures of the Scarlet Pimpernel, Baroness Orczy. A popular sequel to *The Scarlet Pimpernel,* this suspenseful story recounts the Pimpernel's attempts to rescue the Dauphin from imprisonment during the French Revolution. An irresistible blend of intrigue, period detail, and vibrant characterizations. 352pp. 5³⁄₁₆ x 8¼. 0-486-44026-5

ELEGANT SMALL HOMES OF THE TWENTIES: 99 Designs from a Competition, Chicago Tribune. Nearly 100 designs for five- and six-room houses feature New England and Southern colonials, Normandy cottages, stately Italianate dwellings, and other fascinating snapshots of American domestic architecture of the 1920s. 112pp. 9 x 12. 0-486-46910-7

THE ELEMENTS OF STYLE: The Original Edition, William Strunk, Jr. This is the book that generations of writers have relied upon for timeless advice on grammar, diction, syntax, and other essentials. In concise terms, it identifies the principal requirements of proper style and common errors. 64pp. 5⅜ x 8½. 0-486-44798-7

THE ELUSIVE PIMPERNEL, Baroness Orczy. Robespierre's revolutionaries find their wicked schemes thwarted by the heroic Pimpernel — Sir Percival Blakeney. In this thrilling sequel, Chauvelin devises a plot to eliminate the Pimpernel and his wife. 272pp. 5³⁄₁₆ x 8¼. 0-486-45464-9

AN ENCYCLOPEDIA OF BATTLES: Accounts of Over 1,560 Battles from 1479 B.C. to the Present, David Eggenberger. Essential details of every major battle in recorded history from the first battle of Megiddo in 1479 B.C. to Grenada in 1984. List of battle maps. 99 illustrations. 544pp. 6½ x 9¼. 0-486-24913-1

ENCYCLOPEDIA OF EMBROIDERY STITCHES, INCLUDING CREWEL, Marion Nichols. Precise explanations and instructions, clearly illustrated, on how to work chain, back, cross, knotted, woven stitches, and many more — 178 in all, including Cable Outline, Whipped Satin, and Eyelet Buttonhole. Over 1400 illustrations. 219pp. 8⅜ x 11¼. 0-486-22929-7

ENTER JEEVES: 15 Early Stories, P. G. Wodehouse. Splendid collection contains first 8 stories featuring Bertie Wooster, the deliciously dim aristocrat and Jeeves, his brainy, imperturbable manservant. Also, the complete Reggie Pepper (Bertie's prototype) series. 288pp. 5⅜ x 8½. 0-486-29717-9

ERIC SLOANE'S AMERICA: Paintings in Oil, Michael Wigley. With a Foreword by Mimi Sloane. Eric Sloane's evocative oils of America's landscape and material culture shimmer with immense historical and nostalgic appeal. This original hardcover collection gathers nearly a hundred of his finest paintings, with subjects ranging from New England to the American Southwest. 128pp. 10⅝ x 9. 0-486-46525-X

ETHAN FROME, Edith Wharton. Classic story of wasted lives, set against a bleak New England background. Superbly delineated characters in a hauntingly grim tale of thwarted love. Considered by many to be Wharton's masterpiece. 96pp. 5³⁄₁₆ x 8 ¼. 0-486-26690-7

THE EVERLASTING MAN, G. K. Chesterton. Chesterton's view of Christianity — as a blend of philosophy and mythology, satisfying intellect and spirit — applies to his brilliant book, which appeals to readers' heads as well as their hearts. 288pp. 5⅜ x 8½. 0-486-46036-3

THE FIELD AND FOREST HANDY BOOK, Daniel Beard. Written by a co-founder of the Boy Scouts, this appealing guide offers illustrated instructions for building kites, birdhouses, boats, igloos, and other fun projects, plus numerous helpful tips for campers. 448pp. 5³⁄₁₆ x 8¼. 0-486-46191-2

FINDING YOUR WAY WITHOUT MAP OR COMPASS, Harold Gatty. Useful, instructive manual shows would-be explorers, hikers, bikers, scouts, sailors, and survivalists how to find their way outdoors by observing animals, weather patterns, shifting sands, and other elements of nature. 288pp. 5⅜ x 8½. 0-486-40613-X

FIRST FRENCH READER: A Beginner's Dual-Language Book, Edited and Translated by Stanley Appelbaum. This anthology introduces 50 legendary writers — Voltaire, Balzac, Baudelaire, Proust, more — through passages from *The Red and the Black, Les Misérables, Madame Bovary,* and other classics. Original French text plus English translation on facing pages. 240pp. 5⅜ x 8½. 0-486-46178-5

FIRST GERMAN READER: A Beginner's Dual-Language Book, Edited by Harry Steinhauer. Specially chosen for their power to evoke German life and culture, these short, simple readings include poems, stories, essays, and anecdotes by Goethe, Hesse, Heine, Schiller, and others. 224pp. 5⅜ x 8½. 0-486-46179-3

FIRST SPANISH READER: A Beginner's Dual-Language Book, Angel Flores. Delightful stories, other material based on works of Don Juan Manuel, Luis Taboada, Ricardo Palma, other noted writers. Complete faithful English translations on facing pages. Exercises. 176pp. 5⅜ x 8½. 0-486-25810-6

FIVE ACRES AND INDEPENDENCE, Maurice G. Kains. Great back-to-the-land classic explains basics of self-sufficient farming. The one book to get. 95 illustrations. 397pp. 5⅜ x 8½. 0-486-20974-1

FLAGG'S SMALL HOUSES: Their Economic Design and Construction, 1922, Ernest Flagg. Although most famous for his skyscrapers, Flagg was also a proponent of the well-designed single-family dwelling. His classic treatise features innovations that save space, materials, and cost. 526 illustrations. 160pp. 9⅜ x 12¼. 0-486-45197-6

FLATLAND: A Romance of Many Dimensions, Edwin A. Abbott. Classic of science (and mathematical) fiction — charmingly illustrated by the author — describes the adventures of A. Square, a resident of Flatland, in Spaceland (three dimensions), Lineland (one dimension), and Pointland (no dimensions). 96pp. 5³⁄₁₆ x 8¼. 0-486-27263-X

FRANKENSTEIN, Mary Shelley. The story of Victor Frankenstein's monstrous creation and the havoc it caused has enthralled generations of readers and inspired countless writers of horror and suspense. With the author's own 1831 introduction. 176pp. 5³⁄₁₆ x 8¼. 0-486-28211-2

THE GARGOYLE BOOK: 572 Examples from Gothic Architecture, Lester Burbank Bridaham. Dispelling the conventional wisdom that French Gothic architectural flourishes were born of despair or gloom, Bridaham reveals the whimsical nature of these creations and the ingenious artisans who made them. 572 illustrations. 224pp. 8⅜ x 11. 0-486-44754-5

THE GIFT OF THE MAGI AND OTHER SHORT STORIES, O. Henry. Sixteen captivating stories by one of America's most popular storytellers. Included are such classics as "The Gift of the Magi," "The Last Leaf," and "The Ransom of Red Chief." Publisher's Note. 96pp. 5³⁄₁₆ x 8¼. 0-486-27061-0

THE GOETHE TREASURY: Selected Prose and Poetry, Johann Wolfgang von Goethe. Edited, Selected, and with an Introduction by Thomas Mann. In addition to his lyric poetry, Goethe wrote travel sketches, autobiographical studies, essays, letters, and proverbs in rhyme and prose. This collection presents outstanding examples from each genre. 368pp. 5⅜ x 8½. 0-486-44780-4

GREAT EXPECTATIONS, Charles Dickens. Orphaned Pip is apprenticed to the dirty work of the forge but dreams of becoming a gentleman — and one day finds himself in possession of "great expectations." Dickens' finest novel. 400pp. 5³⁄₁₆ x 8¼. 0-486-41586-4

GREAT WRITERS ON THE ART OF FICTION: From Mark Twain to Joyce Carol Oates, Edited by James Daley. An indispensable source of advice and inspiration, this anthology features essays by Henry James, Kate Chopin, Willa Cather, Sinclair Lewis, Jack London, Raymond Chandler, Raymond Carver, Eudora Welty, and Kurt Vonnegut, Jr. 192pp. 5⅜ x 8½. 0-486-45128-3

HAMLET, William Shakespeare. The quintessential Shakespearean tragedy, whose highly charged confrontations and anguished soliloquies probe depths of human feeling rarely sounded in any art. Reprinted from an authoritative British edition complete with illuminating footnotes. 128pp. 5³⁄₁₆ x 8¼. 0-486-27278-8

THE HAUNTED HOUSE, Charles Dickens. A Yuletide gathering in an eerie country retreat provides the backdrop for Dickens and his friends — including Elizabeth Gaskell and Wilkie Collins — who take turns spinning supernatural yarns. 144pp. 5⅜ x 8½. 0-486-46309-5

HEART OF DARKNESS, Joseph Conrad. Dark allegory of a journey up the Congo River and the narrator's encounter with the mysterious Mr. Kurtz. Masterly blend of adventure, character study, psychological penetration. For many, Conrad's finest, most enigmatic story. 80pp. 5³⁄₁₆ x 8¼. 0-486-26464-5

HENSON AT THE NORTH POLE, Matthew A. Henson. This thrilling memoir by the heroic African-American who was Peary's companion through two decades of Arctic exploration recounts a tale of danger, courage, and determination. "Fascinating and exciting." — *Commonweal.* 128pp. 5⅜ x 8½. 0-486-45472-X

HISTORIC COSTUMES AND HOW TO MAKE THEM, Mary Fernald and E. Shenton. Practical, informative guidebook shows how to create everything from short tunics worn by Saxon men in the fifth century to a lady's bustle dress of the late 1800s. 81 illustrations. 176pp. 5⅜ x 8½. 0-486-44906-8

THE HOUND OF THE BASKERVILLES, Arthur Conan Doyle. A deadly curse in the form of a legendary ferocious beast continues to claim its victims from the Baskerville family until Holmes and Watson intervene. Often called the best detective story ever written. 128pp. 5³⁄₁₆ x 8¼. 0-486-28214-7

THE HOUSE BEHIND THE CEDARS, Charles W. Chesnutt. Originally published in 1900, this groundbreaking novel by a distinguished African-American author recounts the drama of a brother and sister who "pass for white" during the dangerous days of Reconstruction. 208pp. 5⅜ x 8½. 0-486-46144-0

THE HUMAN FIGURE IN MOTION, Eadweard Muybridge. The 4,789 photographs in this definitive selection show the human figure — models almost all undraped — engaged in over 160 different types of action: running, climbing stairs, etc. 390pp. 7⅞ x 10⅝. 0-486-20204-6

THE IMPORTANCE OF BEING EARNEST, Oscar Wilde. Wilde's witty and buoyant comedy of manners, filled with some of literature's most famous epigrams, reprinted from an authoritative British edition. Considered Wilde's most perfect work. 64pp. 5³⁄₁₆ x 8¼. 0-486-26478-5

THE INFERNO, Dante Alighieri. Translated and with notes by Henry Wadsworth Longfellow. The first stop on Dante's famous journey from Hell to Purgatory to Paradise, this 14th-century allegorical poem blends vivid and shocking imagery with graceful lyricism. Translated by the beloved 19th-century poet, Henry Wadsworth Longfellow. 256pp. 5³⁄₁₆ x 8¼. 0-486-44288-8

JANE EYRE, Charlotte Brontë. Written in 1847, *Jane Eyre* tells the tale of an orphan girl's progress from the custody of cruel relatives to an oppressive boarding school and its culmination in a troubled career as a governess. 448pp. 5³⁄₁₆ x 8¼.
0-486-42449-9

JAPANESE WOODBLOCK FLOWER PRINTS, Tanigami Kônan. Extraordinary collection of Japanese woodblock prints by a well-known artist features 120 plates in brilliant color. Realistic images from a rare edition include daffodils, tulips, and other familiar and unusual flowers. 128pp. 11 x 8¼. 0-486-46442-3

JEWELRY MAKING AND DESIGN, Augustus F. Rose and Antonio Cirino. Professional secrets of jewelry making are revealed in a thorough, practical guide. Over 200 illustrations. 306pp. 5⅜ x 8½. 0-486-21750-7

JULIUS CAESAR, William Shakespeare. Great tragedy based on Plutarch's account of the lives of Brutus, Julius Caesar and Mark Antony. Evil plotting, ringing oratory, high tragedy with Shakespeare's incomparable insight, dramatic power. Explanatory footnotes. 96pp. 5³⁄₁₆ x 8¼. 0-486-26876-4

Browse over 9,000 books at www.doverpublications.com

THE JUNGLE, Upton Sinclair. 1906 bestseller shockingly reveals intolerable labor practices and working conditions in the Chicago stockyards as it tells the grim story of a Slavic family that emigrates to America full of optimism but soon faces despair. 320pp. 5³⁄₁₆ x 8¼. 0-486-41923-1

THE KINGDOM OF GOD IS WITHIN YOU, Leo Tolstoy. The soul-searching book that inspired Gandhi to embrace the concept of passive resistance, Tolstoy's 1894 polemic clearly outlines a radical, well-reasoned revision of traditional Christian thinking. 352pp. 5³⁄₁₆ x 8¼. 0-486-45138-0

THE LADY OR THE TIGER?: and Other Logic Puzzles, Raymond M. Smullyan. Created by a renowned puzzle master, these whimsically themed challenges involve paradoxes about probability, time, and change; metapuzzles; and self-referentiality. Nineteen chapters advance in difficulty from relatively simple to highly complex. 1982 edition. 240pp. 5⅜ x 8½. 0-486-47027-X

LEAVES OF GRASS: The Original 1855 Edition, Walt Whitman. Whitman's immortal collection includes some of the greatest poems of modern times, including his masterpiece, "Song of Myself." Shattering standard conventions, it stands as an unabashed celebration of body and nature. 128pp. 5³⁄₁₆ x 8¼. 0-486-45676-5

LES MISÉRABLES, Victor Hugo. Translated by Charles E. Wilbour. Abridged by James K. Robinson. A convict's heroic struggle for justice and redemption plays out against a fiery backdrop of the Napoleonic wars. This edition features the excellent original translation and a sensitive abridgment. 304pp. 6⅛ x 9¼.
0-486-45789-3

LILITH: A Romance, George MacDonald. In this novel by the father of fantasy literature, a man travels through time to meet Adam and Eve and to explore humanity's fall from grace and ultimate redemption. 240pp. 5⅜ x 8½.
0-486-46818-6

THE LOST LANGUAGE OF SYMBOLISM, Harold Bayley. This remarkable book reveals the hidden meaning behind familiar images and words, from the origins of Santa Claus to the fleur-de-lys, drawing from mythology, folklore, religious texts, and fairy tales. 1,418 illustrations. 784pp. 5⅜ x 8½. 0-486-44787-1

MACBETH, William Shakespeare. A Scottish nobleman murders the king in order to succeed to the throne. Tortured by his conscience and fearful of discovery, he becomes tangled in a web of treachery and deceit that ultimately spells his doom. 96pp. 5³⁄₁₆ x 8¼. 0-486-27802-6

MAKING AUTHENTIC CRAFTSMAN FURNITURE: Instructions and Plans for 62 Projects, Gustav Stickley. Make authentic reproductions of handsome, functional, durable furniture: tables, chairs, wall cabinets, desks, a hall tree, and more. Construction plans with drawings, schematics, dimensions, and lumber specs reprinted from 1900s The Craftsman magazine. 128pp. 8⅛ x 11. 0-486-25000-8

MATHEMATICS FOR THE NONMATHEMATICIAN, Morris Kline. Erudite and entertaining overview follows development of mathematics from ancient Greeks to present. Topics include logic and mathematics, the fundamental concept, differential calculus, probability theory, much more. Exercises and problems. 641pp. 5⅜ x 8½. 0-486-24823-2

MEMOIRS OF AN ARABIAN PRINCESS FROM ZANZIBAR, Emily Ruete. This 19th-century autobiography offers a rare inside look at the society surrounding a sultan's palace. A real-life princess in exile recalls her vanished world of harems, slave trading, and court intrigues. 288pp. 5⅜ x 8½. 0-486-47121-7

Browse over 9,000 books at www.doverpublications.com

CATALOG OF DOVER BOOKS

THE METAMORPHOSIS AND OTHER STORIES, Franz Kafka. Excellent new English translations of title story (considered by many critics Kafka's most perfect work), plus "The Judgment," "In the Penal Colony," "A Country Doctor," and "A Report to an Academy." Note. 96pp. 5³⁄₁₆ x 8¼.   0-486-29030-1

MICROSCOPIC ART FORMS FROM THE PLANT WORLD, R. Anheisser. From undulating curves to complex geometrics, a world of fascinating images abound in this classic, illustrated survey of microscopic plants. Features 400 detailed illustrations of nature's minute but magnificent handiwork. The accompanying CD-ROM includes all of the images in the book. 128pp. 9 x 9.   0-486-46013-4

A MIDSUMMER NIGHT'S DREAM, William Shakespeare. Among the most popular of Shakespeare's comedies, this enchanting play humorously celebrates the vagaries of love as it focuses upon the intertwined romances of several pairs of lovers. Explanatory footnotes. 80pp. 5³⁄₁₆ x 8¼.   0-486-27067-X

THE MONEY CHANGERS, Upton Sinclair. Originally published in 1908, this cautionary novel from the author of *The Jungle* explores corruption within the American system as a group of power brokers joins forces for personal gain, triggering a crash on Wall Street. 192pp. 5⅜ x 8½.   0-486-46917-4

THE MOST POPULAR HOMES OF THE TWENTIES, William A. Radford. With a New Introduction by Daniel D. Reiff. Based on a rare 1925 catalog, this architectural showcase features floor plans, construction details, and photos of 26 homes, plus articles on entrances, porches, garages, and more. 250 illustrations, 21 color plates. 176pp. 8⅜ x 11.   0-486-47028-8

MY 66 YEARS IN THE BIG LEAGUES, Connie Mack. With a New Introduction by Rich Westcott. A Founding Father of modern baseball, Mack holds the record for most wins — and losses — by a major league manager. Enhanced by 70 photographs, his warmhearted autobiography is populated by many legends of the game. 288pp. 5⅜ x 8½.   0-486-47184-5

NARRATIVE OF THE LIFE OF FREDERICK DOUGLASS, Frederick Douglass. Douglass's graphic depictions of slavery, harrowing escape to freedom, and life as a newspaper editor, eloquent orator, and impassioned abolitionist. 96pp. 5³⁄₁₆ x 8¼.
0-486-28499-9

THE NIGHTLESS CITY: Geisha and Courtesan Life in Old Tokyo, J. E. de Becker. This unsurpassed study from 100 years ago ventured into Tokyo's red-light district to survey geisha and courtesan life and offer meticulous descriptions of training, dress, social hierarchy, and erotic practices. 49 black-and-white illustrations; 2 maps. 496pp. 5⅜ x 8½.   0-486-45563-7

THE ODYSSEY, Homer. Excellent prose translation of ancient epic recounts adventures of the homeward-bound Odysseus. Fantastic cast of gods, giants, cannibals, sirens, other supernatural creatures — true classic of Western literature. 256pp. 5³⁄₁₆ x 8¼.
0-486-40654-7

OEDIPUS REX, Sophocles. Landmark of Western drama concerns the catastrophe that ensues when King Oedipus discovers he has inadvertently killed his father and married his mother. Masterly construction, dramatic irony. Explanatory footnotes. 64pp. 5³⁄₁₆ x 8¼.   0-486-26877-2

ONCE UPON A TIME: The Way America Was, Eric Sloane. Nostalgic text and drawings brim with gentle philosophies and descriptions of how we used to live — self-sufficiently — on the land, in homes, and among the things built by hand. 44 line illustrations. 64pp. 8⅜ x 11.   0-486-44411-2